"Why did you come for me?"

He didn't glance Claudia's way. Never even took his eyes off the road ahead but his hands tightened on the wheel and the tension in his body was contagious. "Because you have something to tell me."

Tomas knew.

Somehow, he'd discovered her condition.

"I'm trying to get my head around what it means, going forward. I took some time to shore up my defenses."

"We'll be married as soon as it can be arranged," he said gruffly.

It wasn't a question, but still... "You want to marry me?"

"Who knows?" He hadn't looked at her once. "But there's a baby coming, so we're doing it. It's the only way."

Kelly Hunter has always had a weakness for fairy tales, fantasy worlds and losing herself in a good book. She has two children, avoids cooking and cleaning and, despite the best efforts of her family, is no sports fan. Kelly is, however, a keen gardener and has a fondness for roses. Kelly was born in Australia and has traveled extensively. Although she enjoys living and working in different parts of the world, she still calls Australia home.

Books by Kelly Hunter

Harlequin Presents

Claimed by a King

Shock Heir for the Crown Prince
Convenient Bride for the King
Untouched Queen by Royal Command
Pregnant in the King's Palace

Billionaires of the Outback

Return of the Outback Billionaire
Cinderella and the Outback Billionaire

Visit the Author Profile page
at Harlequin.com for more titles.

STOLEN PRINCESS'S SECRET

KELLY HUNTER

PRESENTS

H Harlequin®
PRESENTS™

Recycling programs
for this product may
not exist in your area.

ISBN-13: 978-1-335-93910-4

Stolen Princess's Secret

Copyright © 2024 by Kelly Hunter

For questions and comments about the quality of this book, please contact us at CustomerService@Harlequin.com.

TM and ® are trademarks of Harlequin Enterprises ULC.

 Harlequin Enterprises ULC
22 Adelaide St. West, 41st Floor
Toronto, Ontario M5H 4E3, Canada
www.Harlequin.com

Printed in Lithuania

MIX
Paper | Supporting
responsible forestry
FSC® C021394

STOLEN PRINCESS'S SECRET

PROLOGUE

'I'M GOING TO be a falconer when I grow up,' said Claudia, as she watched Tomas offered a sliver of meat to the fierce-eyed peregrine falcon perched on a stand in front of them. 'Just like you.'

'No, you're not,' he corrected, as he curled a soft leather strap around one of the falcon's narrow legs—its metatarsus, his father called it. The falcon, Lolo, was Tomas's first imprint, hand raised by him, and he tended her with every care. His father—the King's Falconer—made sure of it. Tomas gave his second bit of meat to Claudia—positioning it in her little leather-gloved hand *just so* and making sure she held her arm out properly so that Lolo could take it from her with ease. 'You're not allowed.'

'Because I'm a girl?'

'Because you're a princess. Princesses don't get to be falconers.' His eleven-year-old soul was sure of it.

'They do too!'

If he turned, he would see eyes as fierce as any falcon's glaring at him, golden for the most part with a wide rim of dark green around the edges. Those eyes would be accusing, so he kept his attention on Lolo.

First, he fastened the anklets and then the jesses—crafted from a soft brown leather that he'd chosen from the pile and cut into shape beneath his father's watchful gaze. The points were as perfect as he could make them, the greased leather as soft as could possibly be. 'Maybe some of the time you can do falconry,' he allowed. 'In between the princessing.'

'Will *you* be my falconer?' she asked.

'That's the plan.' Both his father and grandfather had been falconers to the royal family of Byzenmaach. 'If I'm good enough.'

'You will be.'

She had a lot of confidence for a little kid. Maybe that was why the birds liked her. She wasn't afraid of their sharp beaks or claws or the fact that above all they were hunters. But she was still careful in their presence—doing exactly what she was told or shown to do, no matter if it was Tomas doing the telling or his father. She looked to him for guidance, and that made him feel big and strong and smart.

Maybe that was why he liked it so much when the little princess gave her tutors the slip and came to visit the falcons.

'There. All done,' he told Lolo. 'Look at you with your new jesses.' She was strong and swift and bred for racing. 'Maybe one day I'll take you to Saudi Arabia to compete in the time trials and you'll win a fine fortune.'

'Can I come too?' Claudia asked. 'What will you do with a fine fortune?'

'Nothing, because it won't be mine.'

'You are correct,' said the gravelly voice of his father

from behind them. 'As much as any bird can be owned, these ones belong to the Crown, along with any prize money they may win.' His gaze fell to Claudia. 'Your governess is looking for you. Again.'

'I guess that means she's awake,' Claudia muttered, her golden eyes downcast. She didn't see the fleeting amusement that crossed his father's face, but Tomas did. His father was a stern man, no point thinking otherwise. But he was fair and never cruel, and there was none better when it came to gaining the trust of wounded animals. He had the touch.

Tomas badly wanted to have the touch too.

'I will escort you into her care,' his father rumbled. 'Tomas, prep enclosure three for incoming when you've finished here.'

Enclosure three was one of their bigger aviaries. 'What are we getting?'

'A mated pair of Steppe eagles.'

'Oh, wow! They're really rare.'

'Indeed.' His father favoured them with one of his rare smiles. 'So put Lolo away and get to work.'

'Yes, Father. Bye, Cl—' His father's quick frown stopped him mid-name. He'd had that lecture about knowing his place and not taking liberties with the young princess's friendship way too many times to want to hear it again. 'Bye, Princess.'

'Are the Steppe eagles coming today?' she asked. 'Do they have names? What do they look like?'

'You will see them tomorrow if your father wills it.' His father spared a meaningful glance for Tomas. 'King

Leonidas and his hunting party arrive this evening. I've let the stable master know.'

Tomas nodded and secured Lolo to her stand. King Leonidas was a cruel man with a vicious temper and a swift arm—especially when he held a riding crop in hand. There were a dozen brood mares grazing the lower valley that would need to go into hiding in the mountains, because what the King did not see he could not ruin. The mares would stay hidden until the King departed, and then Tomas and his father would fly falcons with trailing green ribbon tied to their right legs to signal the all-clear for the stable hands staying with the mares to bring them back down.

Tomas hoped the King and his hunting party didn't stay long.

The light in the little princess's eyes had dimmed at the mention of her father. She too would be kept out of sight during his visit. 'Bye, Tomas, bye, Lolo.' The little girl gave a stiff wave, no bravery left in her, just fear.

His father always told him to make sure an animal felt safe, not scared. It was the biggest rule of all, so how come it never seemed to apply to *this* little girl?

He stepped forward, avoiding his father's gaze as he leaned to whisper in her ear, 'Remember that secret place I showed you?' The secret room in the fortress wall that he'd made his own with candles and hay bales and borrowed blankets and his collection of pretty feathers in an old clay vase. 'Go there if you need to and I'll find you. I'll never rat you out.'

Her lips tightened even as her eyes grew shiny with tears, and then she nodded, once, and flung her arms around his middle and hugged him hard before turning away.

Tomas met his father's hard gaze and squared his shoulders as Claudia set out for the castle. 'She's scared.'

'She has a brother. And a mother. And they are much better placed to withstand a king's wrath than you.' His father's hand on his shoulder was firm. 'You can't encourage her to come to you for comfort, do you understand?'

'Because she's a princess?'

'That, and because if you fall foul of the King, no one will be able to protect you from his wrath. Not even me.'

He shrugged away from his father's hand in a rare display of defiance. It wasn't right for Claudia to be so scared of her father. It wasn't right for her mother to lie in bed day after day and let her children bear an evil king's *wrath*. He didn't even know what the word wrath meant, but he knew what *he* meant whenever he thought of King Leonidas. Vicious, like some of the wild eagles in their care. Vicious and angry and impossible to understand.

'Why can't we ask if Princess Claudia can come here more often and help us with the birds? It would keep her out of sight, just like with the mares. She could imprint one of the peregrine fledglings as part of her lessons, and then she can be here with us more without having to sneak away. What's wrong with that? Can we at least ask for that?'

'You've far too much of your mother in you. Softhearted.'

Tomas's mother had died years ago from a blood cancer that had taken her within weeks of finding out she was sick. Tomas *liked* the thought of being a lot like her. She'd given great hugs and laughed when his hair refused to stay flat. She'd made his father smile and laugh the way no one else ever had. It wasn't wrong to be soft-hearted like her, surely.

'It's just not right that no one keeps a little kid *safe*. Please, Father. Can you ask if she can imprint one of the eyas? It's not a *bad* idea.'

His father bent down until he was at eye level. Hope filled Tomas's body, his soft heart and probably his puppy eyes, as his father nodded slowly. 'I'll try. But you have to promise to leave this to me, understand? You say nothing about wanting to protect her and this being a way to do so. You stay out of trouble and out of sight if her father comes hovering.'

'I promise.' Tomas nodded as hard and as fast as he could.

Days later, his father won permission for Claudia to take falconry lessons, and for a while Tomas's plan worked a treat.

But good intentions didn't always win against evil deeds.

In the end, none of Tomas's fine plans had been enough to keep the little princess safe.

CHAPTER ONE

THERE WAS NOTHING unusual about the cool summer day with the bluest of skies and a fickle wind that ruffled feathers and whipped at his canvas coat. It was just another day in the life of Tomas Sokolov as he stood on the highest battlement of an ancient mountain fortress, with a hawk on his arm. He was the King's Falconer, and he'd been born to this blessed life and he wouldn't have it any other way.

Not for him the life of a nobleman with all its responsibilities and fancy trappings. He didn't particularly like people—apart from one or two who had slipped beneath his skin as a child, and he wasn't drawn to power. Or maybe it was more that when he stepped up to train his eagles and falcons and anything else that came his way, his will was absolute and he liked that a little bit too much. Tomas the tyrant, the dictator, the autocrat. Maybe he *was* drawn to power after all.

Byzenmaach, his homeland, had already seen far too much of that.

But old King Leonidas had passed, and the rule of King Casimir was upon them, and Tomas had no beef with Cas. Better a pragmatic statesman at the helm than a petty madman. Alliances were being built. Prosperity beckoned like a promise. All good, very good, and none of it his responsibility. He had no cause for complaint.

So why, on this fine and perfectly normal afternoon, was he up here looking to the north where the narrow mountain pass brought visitors down onto the plain? Why did restless anticipation ride him so hard?

The hawk knew what was coming her way—the freedom of flight and the hunting of prey. He untethered her, enjoying the look of fierce anticipation in her eyes as she sat perched on his gauntlet.

'Are you ready?' he murmured. 'Maybe you can tell me what's out there.'

Wolves or wolverine, brown bear.

Something.

'What are you doing?'

He didn't need to look over the parapet to know who he would find down there, but he did it anyway. 'You're back.'

At seven years old, young Sophia, newfound daughter of King Casimir, was almost a replica of her late aunt Claudia. She'd been conceived during a brief fling and had spent the first-six years of her life growing up as a normal kid with no knowledge of her father at all. The way Cas told it, he'd certainly had no knowledge of his daughter. Only after Cas had come for her and become engaged to her mother had young Sophia begun to live a life of royalty. Tomas often wondered whether she even liked her new life or whether she missed her old one. Did she enjoy her gilded cage?

She had Claudia's eyes—those remarkable golden

eyes ringed with greeny-grey—along with a child's endless curiosity and tendency to roam the winter fortress with a pair of wolfhounds at her side. She was a sweet child and a bright one, and it wasn't her fault that Tomas could barely look at her without being swamped by unwanted memories of her aunt.

No matter how hard he tried to avoid her, ignore her, and—to his shame—be downright curt with her, she would seek him out. He'd vowed to be kinder and there was no time like the present. Steeling himself, he attempted to assemble his face into something resembling a smile. 'I'm about to fly a hawk. Where are your guards?'

Fortunately, the King was as rabidly protective of his daughter as Tomas could ever hope for. Round-the-clock security had become the norm for those living in and around the winter fortress. Tomas swiftly picked out two heavily armed guards with eyes on the child—one over by the stable door, the other stalking the battlements of the outer wall. There would be a third guard nearby, even if Tomas had yet to sight him.

A heavily armed man stepped out of the shadow of the wall and sketched a brief salute. He was new, and Tomas didn't trust new faces. He was young too. Fresh-faced warriors packed with youthful overconfidence were the worst. 'Master Falconer, may we join you?' he asked.

'If you must.' He sighed as Sophia and her guard made a race towards the outer stairs. It wasn't Sophia's fault Claudia had been snatched away as a child and held for ransom. Claudia's northern captors had wanted a seat at the table when discussing water rights. The King had refused to negotiate and Claudia had died.

Twenty years later, Cas was inviting the northern-ers to finally join the discussion on water rights and, as far as Tomas could tell, Claudia's death had been for nothing.

Sophia had arrived at his side and was trying to hoist herself up on the grey stone wall for a better view, and, 'No,' he growled. Hell, no, she would not sit up there and wriggle and move and give him a heart attack. He moved a few metres to the left, the hawk still perched on his arm as he pointed with his other arm towards a fat stone wedged against the wall. 'You stand on that, and not one part of you is to overreach the wall. You don't lean against it, you don't rest your elbows on the ledge, you don't stick your head over to see how high up you are. Are we clear?'

'Yes, Master Falconer!' Sophia beamed at him.

Why? Why did she have to beam with delight when he was being so stern?

She looked longingly at the hawk but was smart enough not to try and touch her. 'What's her name?'

He'd never known a child so fixated on names. Okay, that wasn't true. He'd known one other who'd been much the same. 'Carys. She's five years old.'

'Will she come back to us if you let her fly free?'

'She's bonded to me so she should return, but there's also a chance she won't.'

'What happens then?'

'We say goodbye and let her go.' He crouched and

rummaged through the pack at his feet for a pair of binoculars. 'Do you know how to use these?'

'Yes!'

He handed them to her just as a high-pitched whistle sounded on the outer battlements. Two more short sharp whistles had guards converging and pointing to the north. Sophia, too, had the binoculars to her eyes and trained towards the north. It probably wouldn't be right to snatch those binoculars back, but only iron-clad control stopped him from doing so regardless.

'There's a lady on a horse,' said Sophia. 'Dressed in, like, furs. And a man on another horse and two wolfhounds.'

'Which way are they riding?'

'This way.'

He had the oddest feeling. A thundering in his heart that he couldn't explain.

'Give the master falconer his binoculars back, youngling,' said the guard. 'And crouch down.'

Tomas had never been more grateful. 'There's a purple silk ribbon in my pack. Find it for me.' Keeping Sophia occupied was only part of that directive. Compulsion rode him now, as he focused on the riders. It was as she said. Two riders, two wolfhounds, two horses. And there was something about the dark-haired woman that turned his blood to ice.

No.

But what if?

She's dead, he argued to himself.

They never got her body back.

She's been confirmed dead for twenty years.

He'd been there the day she'd been taken by a guard who was supposed to protect her. He'd seen them in the garden. He'd thought nothing of it, and for years he'd blamed himself for not noticing that something was wrong. If only he'd been more observant. If only he'd waved to Claudia and called her over rather than hurrying after his father because he wasn't supposed to be friends with her when other people were looking... If only he'd done something *different*.

No one had ever seen her again.

He crouched down beside Sophia as she pulled the strip of royal purple silk from the bag. 'You know what this is?'

She shook her head, no.

'It's an old method of communication that falconers sometimes use when they fly their birds.' He wasn't even sure why he'd brought the silk with him in the first place, other than he'd been battling a memory of him and Claudia lying in front of his father's fire with a fragile book spread out in front of him that listed all the colours a royal raptor could fly and what they meant. He'd been the one reading, as usual. Claudia had been listening like a little sponge. 'When I attach it to Carys's right leg, like this, it means royalty is in residence and it offers incoming visitors royal protection.'

'Er, Master Falconer, sir, are you at liberty to be offering that?'

'Too late.' He lifted his arm and Carys shot into the sky. 'There are only half a dozen people alive who even know what that ribbon means.' So why was he flying that ribbon at all? Instinct?

Instinct and false, fierce hope, and a thundering heart.

Word went around the fortress that they had incoming visitors and curiosity grew. Visitors heading in from the high mountain pass, on horseback, was unusual. Carys had spotted the riders and was heading towards them. Nothing strange about that. He'd trained her to mark the presence of large animals.

And then the woman dismounted, pulled a gauntlet from her saddlebag and called that bird straight out of the sky.

His bird.

Using his signals.

It *couldn't* be.

But what if it was?

He could feel the blood draining from his face, leaving him clammy and shaken. Had there not been an audience, he would have sunk to his heels and leaned against the wall and taken strength from the only home he'd ever known. As it was, he had to put his hand to the wall to steady himself.

'Sophia, go get Housemaster Silas and tell him to get up here.' Silas and his wife Lor had managed the running of the fortress for decades. Out of anyone, he might, *might*, hear Tomas out.

Ten long minutes later he met the gaze of an out of breath Silas, and avoided looking at Sophia's mother— the soon-to-be Queen Consort Ana—and tried to project calm confidence as he explained the calling of his bird from the sky situation.

'So she's a falconer too,' said Ana.

'He thinks it's Claudia,' said Silas, his weary old eyes fixed on Tomas with unwavering intensity.

'I didn't *say* that,' Tomas protested.

'But you think it,' Silas replied.

'Just to be clear, you're talking Claudia, as in Casimir's dead sister?' Ana looked from one man to the other. 'You're serious.'

'We never got her body back,' Tomas said stubbornly.

'We got some of it back,' countered Silas.

'Okay,' said Ana hurriedly. 'Small girl on the battlements. Listening.'

Tomas felt himself flush. Silas shut his eyes and shook his head.

'Is there any way we can get a look at the woman's face?' Ana said next.

'She's wearing traditional headdress. Only part of her face is showing. It could be anyone.'

'But you think it's her.'

'I don't *know*.' Tomas swore and turned away before his control deserted him. Swearing in front of women and children, what next? '*She* knew about the coloured cloth instead of jesses and what they meant. It's in one of the royal falconry journals and I read that section aloud to her when she was helping me nurse a hawk with a broken wing. She was good with the birds. They trusted her. She knew all our call signals.'

'Why would she stay away all these years, only to return now?' asked Silas.

'Who knows?' Tomas snapped but he could take a wild guess. 'Because her father who left her to rot is dead, her brother is whole and happy, Byzenmaach is moving forward and she wants to come home? How should I know?'

'But you think it's her,' said Ana. 'Again, just to be clear.'

He stared at her and then Silas and finally young Sophia, with those eyes so wide and round. He didn't know. He couldn't be sure. But here he was staking his reputation and likely his livelihood on the return of a woman from the dead.

'Yes.'

'Then we have to tell Cas.'

The winter fortress stood exactly as she remembered it, starkly grey against a brilliant blue sky. Built into the side of a cliff face, there would be no attacking it from the south, just endless views over a secluded valley several thousand feet below. To the far north, and behind her now, rose a vast mountain range, inaccessible to all but the hardiest of mountain clans. Between mountain and fortress lay flat unwooded plains—a battleground of old with no place to hide. They would be seen. They *had* been seen—the hawk currently perched on her arm confirmed it.

A hawk carrying a strip of purple cloth.

Welcome, that strip of cloth said, if she remembered correctly. *We see you and you may approach. We offer our protection.*

She'd given no notice regarding her arrival. Who would believe her identity without seeing her in the flesh? And even then, she had her doubts as to whether anyone would know her on sight. So many years had passed. Her features had changed so much.

All she could hope for was an audience with someone who'd once known her.

Her brother, ideally, if he was in residence.

Silas and Lor, the older couple who had once managed the fortress, if they still served.

Tomas.

The bird on her arm spoke of his presence.

Or maybe she was just being hopeful.

'First smile I've seen from you in a week,' murmured her companion. Having Ildris by her side on this journey was a comfort, because he was a big brother to her in all ways that mattered, and twelve years older than she was. It gave him an aura of strength and maturity, those two words describing him perfectly.

'Coming home's a scary business,' she replied, pulling two ribbons from her saddlebag. White for peace. Purple for royalty. What a beautiful hawk to sit so patiently on her gauntlet and let her attach coloured ribbons to the left anklet. The ribbons hinted at who she was and what her intentions were. The King's Falconer would surely know what they meant. It was his job.

'It could have been less fraught for all concerned had you allowed me to inform them of your return,' Ildris offered dryly.

'Who would believe you?'

'I think you just like creating drama.'

He wasn't exactly *wrong*.

'Then let's just say I've waited so long for this day, and it serves many purposes to claim the element of surprise. In that first moment of recognition, we'll be able to tell allies from enemies. And there will be enemies. Hopefully, my brother won't be one of them.' Her blood brother, Casimir, had grown to manhood beneath their father's cruel yoke. Who knew what kind of man he'd become?

Ildris sat comfortably in the saddle as she finished tying the ribbons and launched the hawk into the sky. 'What do you remember of him?'

'I have so many memories based on fear of my father and my mother's neglect, but Cas…he tried so hard to protect me. He took the lash for me, over and over again.' She shook her head to clear her mind of those bitter memories. 'One of my greatest regrets is not being able to tell him I was alive and happy. I don't know how that's going to go.'

'Tell him that no matter our initial intent, once your father refused to negotiate your return, you were safe with us. Tell him we nurtured you and love you. We are not forcing your return—you could have stayed with us for ever. This time, we could and *would* have negotiated without involving you.'

'I know.' And she loved him and the council of the northern clans all the more for making that clear. 'But I *want* to help him and his new wife and their little girl who looks just like me when I was her age. I want Byzenmaach to move forward. I truly want to serve my country and I'm uniquely positioned to do so. You always thought I'd return one day. You took me in and built me for exactly this moment.'

'Do you really think that?' he grumbled. 'My parents

took you in because they were never on board with taking a child hostage. We gave you political survival skills so that no one would take advantage of you. Does it also not stand to reason that I'm wary of returning you to those who once considered you expendable?'

'I don't think my brother ever thought me expendable.'

'I hope you're right. Otherwise, we're in a bit of trouble. Yet another reason for telling people about you from a safe distance. The *trust* involved in expecting them to greet you with joy rather than suspicion. I shudder.'

'You're loving this.' She remounted and they continued on their way. 'You live for excitement.'

'*Live* being the operative word.'

'It's going to be fine. Cas has already reached out to the northern clans in peace. What better measure of good faith negotiation than the return of one of Byzenmaach's beloved jewels? And by that I mean me.'

For good or for ill, she was coming home and fully prepared to wield any scrap of power her identity afforded her.

'I'm ready, Ildris. For whatever comes next.' She watched the hawk soar, ribbons trailing, and hoped that if the owner of the hawk was Tomas, that he had not forgotten her. That he, of all people, would keep an open heart and mind. She had such sweet memories of him.

His boyish face in the firelight. His youthful voice as he'd stumbled over unfamiliar words as he read from books way too advanced for him. His hidey-holes and his smiles when he was absolutely certain no one else was looking.

It would take more than a lifetime before she ever forgot the fine mind and tender heart of her very first friend.

It took the riders what seemed like half a lifetime but in reality was measured by hours before they reached the outer walls of the fortress. There they had dismounted to shed layers of clothing and weapons. Rifles and scimitars, daggers and even the woman's hairpins. A dark plait had fallen to her waist in the absence of those lethal fasteners. She'd turned slowly in a circle, her arms out wide and her movements graceful. She and her companion were stating with vivid clarity that they were entering unarmed.

The stately, ceremonial nature of their approach had set people on edge. Cas had arrived by helicopter. Sophia had been safely stashed away inside the fortress and security was on full alert. The mysterious travellers were making their final approach, on foot, towards the stable doors.

'Let them come,' Casimir had commanded. 'No one is to ride out to meet them.'

The tension behind Tomas's eyes was excruciating. What were they even *doing*, adhering so closely to the old ways when they had all sorts of technology that could help to identify them without actually letting them in? It was as if time had slowed and hope had risen and reason had unequivocally left the building.

The stables were as they'd ever been. Twenty stalls capable of holding three or four horses apiece ran either side of a large central square. The square was covered in sawdust and the stable hands kept it immaculate. Huge wooden doors stood sentry on opposite sides of the square. Doors strong enough to hold invaders out rather than horses in.

Tomas stood in the centre of the sawdust square alongside Ana, with Cas on her other side. The stable master, stable hands and a company of guards took up other positions as Cas finally ordered the opening of the outer doors to let the visitors in.

The male rider entered first, leading his horse. He picked Casimir out of the crowd and steadily approached.

'Your Majesty,' he said with the click of his heels and a swift bow. 'It's been a long time.'

'Welcome, Lord Ildris of the North.' Cas clearly knew the man by sight, even if Tomas didn't. 'Who's your companion?'

The northerner waited a beat, as if taking a deep breath. 'She's the negotiator you requested and speaks for the people of the north and for herself. A future for a future, Your Majesty. Delivered to you in good faith.'

The woman entered the stables, swift and sure, and the horses and dogs followed, and Tomas knew who she was even before she lifted her eyes and made it a foregone conclusion. Her eyes were the same shape and colour as Casimir's. Same as Sophia's. The eyes of the royal family of Byzenmaach.

'Hello, Cas,' she offered quietly and then her gaze flickered sideways, passing over Ana to rest squarely on him. 'And Tomas. You're the falconer here now?'

He had no words. He could barely remember to

breathe, so it was fortunate that Ana answered for him. 'Yes, he is.'

'I thought so.' She smiled as if they'd just shared a joke, but he could find no smile for her in return. He was too busy fighting a horde of emotions that threatened to overwhelm him. Astonishment. Disbelief. Anger. Relief. Where had she *been* these past twenty years or more?

And then Ana said something to Cas in Russian and then Cas was striding across the floor and pulling his sister into an embrace that left no one in any doubt of the depth of his supposed loss, or his joy at finding her alive.

'You were right, Tomas,' Ana murmured, and maybe he should have stuck around but he'd had enough of this day and all the drama, and if he was going to break down, he wanted to do it in private.

He turned on his heel and left without a word. Back to the house he'd been born and raised in, shedding his clothes as he headed for the shower and the tap that brought the icy underground river water into the homes of those living here, to be heated by a furnace and pushed through pipes so it could beat down on a man's head, hot and strong or icy cold and anything in between. A pleasure or a punishment, and today he chose the latter, standing beneath the stinging, icy spray far longer than was wise in an effort to wash away his confusion.

Claudia of Byzenmaach was *dead*. He'd *mourned* her. They all had. Her absence had coloured their lives.

Did the impossibly beautiful woman who stood there, so regal and composed, have *any* idea of the sorrow she'd left behind? Where had she been all those years?

What atrocities had she endured? And to single him out. To remember his name and greet him like an old friend. She'd stood, magnificent and defiant, so impossibly alive and begging him with her eyes to acknowledge her existence…

Emotion after emotion broke over him. Confusion. Resentment. Rage. Where was it all coming from?

He didn't *want* to be drowning in emotions. *Get a grip.*

He was a man of firm control, not seething, unruly compulsions. A simple man, a falconer. Nothing more and nothing less. There would be no befriending the returned princess of Byzenmaach. No trying to protect her, no welcoming her home. *Definitely* no regarding her as an impossibly desirable woman capable of setting his body alight at a glance. He wanted nothing to do with her. Nothing!

He was *not* getting caught up in Princess Claudia of Byzenmaach's blast radius ever again.

CHAPTER TWO

CLAUDIA COULDN'T SLEEP, and it had nothing to do with the warm and heartfelt reception she'd received from her brother and his family. Maybe it had something to do with the adrenaline-filled day and the capture of her senses as she'd built new memories over old ones and tracked all the changes that had occurred to people and possessions. Mostly, her wakefulness had to do with a certain falconer with an impossibly beautiful masculine face, eyes of darkest brown and stern lips that spoke of sensuality under rigid control.

Tomas had been standing there with Ana and Cas as she'd entered the stables and he'd known who she was in an instant. She'd seen it in his eyes—a kaleidoscope of feelings she hadn't possibly been able to decipher in such a short time before her attention had been forced elsewhere.

'The one who left the stables first is not your friend,' Ildris had told her just before bed, right before he'd withdrawn to his guestroom, and maybe that assessment was keeping her awake too.

Because Claudia absolutely disagreed with Ildris on that point. She stood at the bedroom window, staring out

at the faint light in the building on the edge of the fortress that had once housed fledgling falcons and probably still did.

In all her reckonings of how this day would unfold,
Tomas welcoming her home had always been part of it.
A constant amidst ever changing variables. He would
know who she was at a glance and would be overjoyed
to see her alive and well and…

Well…

Apart from knowing who she was at a glance, reality really hadn't delivered.

And that light in his window was beckoning and it
wasn't as if she was sleepy.

Donning her travelling cloak and nodding to the pair
of guards stationed just outside the bedroom door, Claudia made her way through the corridors of the fortress
to the kitchen and from there to the herb garden and
the deep shadows of battlement walls. She was being
watched, no doubt, but she couldn't be caring about that.
There was only so much space in her mind to begin with
and at the moment it was full of Tomas the boy overlaid
with an image of Tomas the man, and her overwhelming
desire to make things right between them. Their friendship had existed in the shadows all those years ago, and
in the shadows she hoped to find it again.

She knocked on the wooden door to the falconer's
workspace with every good intention and a dozen expla-
nations on her lips, but when the door opened to allow
her entry and Tomas turned without a word and stalked
away from her down the narrow entry hall, speech deserted her. He was a presence. An unknown force, bat-

tering away at her senses. Too big to make sense of, his shoulders too broad. Too stern. Ever so silent.

She followed him anyway.

He led her to what had once been the falcon nursery. These days it seemed to be an office with a couple of perches but no falcons currently present.

He took a seat behind the desk and motioned to the chair on the other side, all without saying a word. She had a feeling he could sit here all night, eyes stony and lips tight.

'Hi,' she murmured.

Icebreaker it was not.

She tried again. 'I'm guessing you have questions.'

'No.'

Oh. 'Because anything you want to know, I'll answer you. I mean, if you really want the deep dive into what happened we'll be here for days, but I could cover the basics quickly enough.'

Curiosity flared briefly in those assessing dark eyes. Curiosity and an internal conversation he seemed to be having with himself before he finally allowed himself a single slight nod. 'Then cover the basics.'

'Right.' It wasn't much of an invitation but it was enough. 'I got kidnapped from the palace by northerners hoping to force water concessions from my father. That didn't work. They wanted to return me. That didn't work either.'

His eyes narrowed. 'Why not? Why couldn't they have just given you back?'

'Because I was in the room when my father told them he didn't want me back. As far as he was concerned, I was damaged goods and better martyred than returned. He said that if they let me go, he'd kill me himself and blame it on them anyway. Is that a good enough reason to stay away until now, do you think?'

He had the most magnificent scowl.

'This presented a problem for my captors who, apart from the whole kidnapping thing, had treated me well enough up until that point. What were they going to do with me?'

'Tell me.'

She did like *this* Tomas's voice commands. He'd grown into his authority quite magnificently.

'A wealthy clan who'd voted against the abduction petitioned the council to think of me as an abandoned child and put me up for adoption. The council agreed, so the family took me in and gave me every opportunity to grow up strong and whole. I wasn't abused by them or anyone else.' She'd had to reassure Cas of this several times over and figured Tomas might appreciate similar emphasis. 'My father died, Cas wants to negotiate water rights with the northerners, finally giving them a seat at the table, and here I am. I know it won't be easy, fitting back in, but I can honestly say that so far it feels good to be home.'

'Your brother must be overjoyed.'

'I hope so. Are you glad to see me too? Because I really can't tell. Ildris thinks you're no friend of mine. I say you are.'

'Is this *Ildris* an abductor of children? Or is he of the clan of opportunists who took you in? Either way, I have no time at all for what he thinks.'

'Remind me never to seat you two beside one another at the dinner table.'

Savage little smirk from him at her words. 'Never going to happen.'

Civilised behaviour seemed to sit only lightly on this man. Boy Tomas had been softer.

Maybe if she stopped mapping every curve and plane of his face for traces of the child he'd once been, she could concentrate more on breaking the ice with him, although, to be fair, he was studying her just as closely.

'And you? I heard about your father's death in the papers and that you'd taken over here and were doing good things. You've been well? Life is treating you well?'

I never forgot you, she wanted to say. *I thought of you so many times. I never factored in that meeting you again would involve me wanting to fling myself into your arms, but here we are.*

Probably best not to mention any of that right now.

'I knew you'd grow up to be a falconer, of course.' Small talk was her friend. 'I did think you'd talk more and scowl less, but maybe you're just shy.'

'I'm not shy.'

'Standoffish, then, but that's okay too. I haven't forgotten any of your kindnesses. I'd like us to be friends again.' Start small. Build from there.

'I see.' He nodded as if they'd reached an accord. 'No, that's not going to happen.'

She reached out instinctively, her hand over his, and felt the sting of attraction rip through her skin and into her veins. He swiftly withdrew his hand from beneath hers and his eyes flashed fierce warning before he shielded them with long black lashes.

'What was that?' She knew exactly what it was, but did he?

'Nothing.'

'Then you won't mind if we try it again.' She held out her hand for him to shake, put it right in his line of sight. 'Hi, I'm Claudia.'

'No.'

'No to a simple handshake?'

'It's not a handshake. It's not simple. I'm not the boy you used to know.'

Maybe she needed a different approach.

'You should know that I don't give up on people easily. I'm *so* used to not being wanted at first glance. At second glance too. Even at tenth glance. I'm very persistent.'

'That's okay,' he murmured, echoing some of her earlier words with a smile that made ice look warm. 'You may be persistent but I'm as stubborn as they come. If you need someone to drive a team of oxen up a mountain, I'm your man. If I can be of service to you in any official or professional capacity, I will be. But I don't weather surprises well and I hate messy emotions and right now you're blasting both at me. I'm glad you're back, don't get me wrong. Surprised as hell, but glad you're alive and relieved your captivity wasn't terrible. God knows I never wanted you dead. But I don't have the time or the inclination to renew old friendships or go tripping down memory lane with you. I hope you can understand my position.'

'I don't understand your position.'

'What a shame. Maybe understanding will come to you in time. Now, if you don't mind, Princess, it's almost three a.m. and I have a sick falcon to see to. He stood and she looked up, up into pitiless eyes. 'You know the way out.'

Well, damn. Ildris had been right.

The King's Falconer was proving elusive.

Again.

In the three months she'd been back she'd caught up with the falconer only a handful of times, and every time he'd remained perfectly, excruciatingly polite and completely closed off to her overtures of friendship. This didn't stop her returning to the winter fortress whenever Cas could spare her, though. She loved it here on the edge of a cliff face, with her beloved mountain in the distance and a chill in the air even on the sunniest days. And this time she'd come armed with a missive from the King, all signed, sealed and soon to be delivered.

To Tomas.

Lor said he was in residence.

Her interest in the royal racing falcons and breeding and rehabilitation programmes was real, no need to pretend. She might not have the experience Tomas's apprentices were getting, but she had enough knowledge to ask sensible questions and be of use when it came to handling the raptors currently in royal care. Not that anyone ever let her help. They were under strict instructions not to let anyone near their charges without the King's Falconer's approval.

She'd tried asking nicely, but he'd been on his way to collect a falcon. Bad timing, he'd said.

She'd put her request to have access to the aviaries in writing and received no reply.

Third time lucky, right?

In her hand she carried yet another request for her to have access to the aviaries and this time the request came from Cas. Tomas—if he had a subversive bent, which he absolutely *did*—could deny he'd ever received such a request if she didn't deliver it to him personally, so here she was, about to do exactly that.

She'd warned him she was persistent.

Claudia found him in a white-walled office crammed with filing cabinets along one wall and several computers set up haphazardly on any available surface. He sat behind a corner desk with a phone to his ear and a frown on his face that deepened when he saw her. He didn't motion for her to sit, but she placed the letter dead centre on his desk and swivelled it so that his name on the envelope was facing him, fully aware that he was watching her every move.

She'd spent a ridiculous amount of time on her hair and make-up this morning. She'd tried on three different sets of outdoor 'work' clothes. She'd armoured up in preparation to see him again because apparently she was perfectly capable of having a crush on him with all the avid obsession of a hormonal thirteen-year-old.

What joy.

Smiling tightly, she then turned her back on him and proceeded to poke around his office.

Okay, not poke, she wasn't quite that rude, maybe

prowl was the description she needed. There was a wall of bird photographs, with names neatly printed beneath each image. Once she'd inhaled all that, she memorised the weekly roster and the names and duties of his apprentices. And of course she listened to his side of the phone conversation.

'I don't have any room,' he said more than once. 'We're full. I know. Leave it with me. I'll call you back.' Two more rapid phone calls, one to France, the other to Latvia, and he was indeed calling that first person back and giving them the contact details of the raptor sanctuary he'd organised to take their breeding pair of endangered goshawks. Finally, he put the phone down and stared at her.

She'd been waiting over twenty minutes.

'Hello,' she murmured now that she had his full attention. She was certainly prepared to offer him all of hers in return. 'Good job on rehoming the goshawks.'

She loved the way he exuded healthy masculinity in his rough labourer's clothes that included wide leather bands wrapped casually around both forearms. Muscles bulged. Angels sighed. Falconers had an unfair advantage when it came to looking effortlessly sexy. Not that she was inclined to mention it. She was all about keeping this meeting professional. Mostly professional. She'd see how she went.

'Are you the president of some kind of raptor relocation outfit?'

'No.' He gestured towards the envelope. 'What's this?'

'Another request for access to the royal aviaries. I've

also included my falconry experience, starting from age seven. It's extensive.'

His eyes narrowed as he stared at her—a suspicious-hearted person might have even called it a glare. And then he turned his attention to the envelope, discarding Cas's covering letter after a swift glance in favour of scanning her C.V.

Quite voraciously. It was very gratifying.

'It says here you're a Master Falconer.'

Claudia beamed.

'Where are your birds?'

'Still in the mountains. And while I'd happily bring them here, I'm currently busy taming Cas's courtiers, and it sounds like you don't have room to keep them. I'd like to discuss it though, just in case you can find some way to accommodate them.'

'There's an onboarding process for anyone wanting access to the royal aviaries,' he said.

'Of course.' She expected no less. 'And I am here for it. Are you free now?'

She'd ambushed him, used her position to corner him, and he didn't know whether to be resentful or impressed. Just another set of opposing emotions to add to the collection he carried deep within whenever he thought of her. And with the newspapers and magazines and fortress gossip fair bursting with talk of the political demands she was making and the family gowns and tiaras she was wearing, not to mention her ever growing influence over her brother and his family, he thought about the returned princess of Byzenmaach *plenty*.

She didn't even have to be *present*.

'I'm here for the next two days and I'd really like to get my onboarding on track,' she was saying, and he seriously considered making it happen.

Maybe if he onboarded her himself, he could form his own opinion on the type of person she'd grown up to be and stop buying into all the gossip she created just by breathing in a particular direction. He could stop watching the many television interviews she'd taken to giving, because they downright did his head in. It was impossible not to admire her grit, even as he wondered what the hell she thought she was *doing*, dabbling in political minefields that were minefields for a reason.

'Let's do it now,' he said of the onboarding, choosing for once to step up and wear the emotional turmoil of connection.

Go him. Such outreach. His former girlfriends would hardly recognise him.

'Really?'

Don't beam at me. Don't shine like you've just won the lottery.

'Yes.'

She beamed at him, and he scowled right back because the world needed balance.

But he gave her the respect her qualifications deserved and took her on a comprehensive tour, the VIP colleague version, and she was knowledgeable, enthusiastic and full of praise. She cooed over his rare mating pairs. Told a featherless but talkative parrot he was her new favourite, and when they entered the aviary full of peregrine falcons and he handed her gloves and a bucket of feed she proved herself more than capable of feeding them by hand in orderly fashion.

She kept enough physical distance from him to render him comfortable, right up until they rounded a bend outside aviary three and she lost her footing on a slippery rock step and he shot out his hand to steady her. These paths could be dangerous, especially when covered in late afternoon shade.

'Sorry,' she murmured, righting herself. 'Slippery.'

He probably should have anticipated the sudden pounding of his heart—either from touching her or at the thought of her falling. Nothing to do with sexual attraction at all. Probably.

'Give me your shoe size and I'll order some boots in with rubber tread like mine.'

'You'd do that for me?'

'I do that for everyone who works for me. Not that you do work for me or that I expect you to. But if you want unlimited, unsupervised access to the aviaries, you may as well have all the gear.'

'And will you allow me that access?'

'Yes.'

Her eyes lit up, the same way they always had done when they'd been kids and she'd done well and been praised for it. Made him want to preen. Made him a little too slow to drop his hand and withdraw that physical support. More fool him.

He'd embarked on project *Make Claudia Welcome* in an effort to get over her, not to become ever more in thrall to the woman.

By the time they got back to his office, the sun had

slid behind the distant mountain range and shadows painted the ground. He scanned the clipboard on his desk, and the long list of tasks and ticks and the comments column for anything in need of his attention. She was still there. Still eager to know everything.

'You've expanded so much. It's brilliant! Imagine what you could do with more resources,' Claudia was saying.

If only.

And why was she still here? They'd said their farewells five minutes ago, hadn't they?

'Do you want more resources?' she asked perceptively.

'Your brother and I have discussed it.' Tomas hoped that with their recent speed trial wins that they might take another look at avian resources, but it hadn't happened yet. Cas was busy, not least with reining in his long lost and in no way dead sibling. 'It'll happen eventually.' He wanted to believe it. 'Your brother means well.'

'Damned by faint praise,' she murmured.

'But it is praise. Your father's rule was…difficult. People are understandably wary, and your brother has yet to prove himself. I know what you're doing, by the way. Making *your* views the target of political outrage when anyone with a brain knows they're your brother's views as well. Nice little sidestep he's got going there. Letting you take all the heat.'

'Careful, Tomas. I'll start to think you're a political being.'

'Never. Spare me the company of craven courtiers. I hate them all.' He meant it.

'And yet my brother speaks very highly of your ability to deal with them.'

'I serve as I ever have.'

Claudia snorted, and even that managed to sound fetching. 'I certainly hope not. From memory, you and your father and the rest of the staff here were extremely adept at limiting my father's impact on the world around him.'

He grunted in reply. No point incriminating himself or others.

'So what do you think of the water rights treaty?' she asked. 'It's exciting, right? With conservation at the forefront and guaranteed access for those who need it.'

Always with the questions, luring him into unwanted conversation.

'As you say, things are changing, and people are hopeful.'

He watched her cross to the picture board with the names of all the falcons on it. She'd been captivated by that earlier too. He usually asked new apprentices to memorise it within a week. Instinct told him it wouldn't take her that long.

'Do you still think we can't be friends?' she asked quietly.

'You're a princess, I'm a servant.'

'Oh, c'mon,' she scoffed. 'We did away with that distinction twenty years ago.'

'We certainly did *not*.'

'In private we did.' When had she become all angles and impossible beauty? So utterly compelling? He didn't want to be her friend, that still hadn't changed. But since when had he wanted lovers' rights? A fully adult and possibly X-rated relationship? Had he come to that conclusion five minutes ago? Ten? Was the feather-less parrot to blame?

Because he really wanted to blame *something* for his appalling lack of judgement.

'If you want access to the royal aviaries, you have it.' Time to get this briefing back on track. 'If you let me know how many birds you want to bring in I'll make space for them, even if we have to house them in the fortress proper—we've done that before and we can cer-tainly do it for you. They'll need vet checks and a clean bill of health before they arrive and I'll send you an in-formation questionnaire that needs to be filled out for each bird. If you can't take them to the palace when you go there to be your brother's political scapegoat—which I don't agree with, by the way, he's doing you no favours by letting you take point—I'll put them in my personal flight rotation. I'll even give you updates. Just don't ask me to send pictures of them with little voice bubbles or videos with them dancing to music or wearing cowboy hats and neck ties, because I won't do it. Is that a good enough extension of the hand of friendship?'

'Well, when you put it like that,' she said, golden eyes shining, holding out her hand for him to shake, and damn her for making his pulse spike again. 'I'll take it.'

Claudia spent the rest of the evening riding a wave of happiness. She had dinner with Silas and Lor in the big kitchen, with her wolfhounds at her feet and Sophia's as well. Casimir had kept the wolfhound name traditions going. The heavily pregnant wolfhound stretched out in front of the huge stone hearth was Jelly Belly the eleventh. Or was she the twelfth?

Coming home had been harder than expected. She'd ridden in with a heart full of hope that she would be accepted and a deeply buried fear that she would prove useful to no one. Not the northerners, who expected so much from her bulldozer-style advocacy. Not her brother, whose rule had invariably become more complicated upon her return.

She needed to succeed in all her roles. She needed to be strong and powerful, politically invaluable, and above all confident. Make Cas look good. Take the extreme position if she had to so that he could swoop in with a more moderate stance and yet still make ample progress. That was the plan. Her only plan.

But Tomas had clocked it and criticised her actions and she too had underestimated just how much courage it would take to face suspicion and outright hostility from the select few politicians who, first and foremost, were still her father's men. Cruel, powerful men with years of alliances and information to trade upon. Ugly business, the ruling of worlds. Corruption never far from the centre.

She hadn't factored in how much energy it would take to keep her emotional armour permanently in place, and her reserves were wearing thin.

Tomas's friendship, or whatever he wanted to call it, was a godsend.

Her mobile rang and she glanced at the screen for the name of the caller.

Cas.

'Brother! You rang?'

'I did. How did it go with Tomas?'

'I like to think I wowed him with my poise, maturity and falcon-feeding skills and maybe even reclaimed the threads of an old and valuable friendship. The reality is probably a lot less rosy, but progress has been made, which makes me happy.'

She could almost see her brother picking over her words, analysing her good humour, and coming to conclusions.

'I never realised how close you and Tomas were as children.'

'He was safety,' she offered simply.

'How did I not know this?'

'*Secret* safety.'

'And now what is he?'

'Who knows?' A reluctant champion? Her latest late-night fantasy? Definitely the latter. 'He's incredibly hard to read. All that iron control, and I know he needs it for his birds, but it's annoying. Cas, stop laughing. It's not helpful.'

Her brother did stop laughing. Eventually. 'He's not an easy man to know, our master falconer. By all accounts, he's a demanding but fair teacher. He's not a fan of small talk. He could barely stand to be in the same room as Sophia when she first arrived. I believe it was because she reminded him so strongly of you. Now she tracks him down whenever she visits and his patience with her is a sight to behold.'

'I refuse to feel jealous of my niece,' she told him loftily. 'Even if I am.'

'Tomas knew you had returned the moment you rode into this valley. The facts were all against it. He could barely bring himself to voice the words lest everyone think him a madman, but he knew it was you. Ana will tell you that he never truly released you from his heart, even though everybody said you were dead, but that's just…wild.'

Yes, it was.

'I'd love to see him with the capacity to expand his role beyond being merely your falconer. He's worth investing in.'

'*Merely* the King's Falconer? Is that not exalted enough?'

'He needs more resources. Would you like to hear my plan?'

'Perhaps. But first I have a question. What is it you want from him? Not *for* him. *From* him.'

She thought long and hard before answering. 'I want him to feel more comfortable around me than he currently does. I want him to like me.' There it was. 'And I can't get it out of my head that he's hurting because of me. Because I left. Because I'm back. Because I didn't write to say *hi, I'm still alive.* I don't know *why* my presence pains him, but it does. All I can do is guess.'

'And guess badly,' Cas admonished.

'Maybe if he thought of me growing up at all, he imagined someone different from who I turned out to be. Maybe I'm a disappointment. Not worth spending time on.'

There it was, her primal fear revealed—nurtured by years upon years of having to justify her existence.

'What if it's that?'

'It's not. *You* are a survivor. You're smart and strong and incisive and caring and open. And you could have turned out differently after all you've been through. You could have been hard-hearted and resentful, suspicious and untrusting, and no one would blame you, but you're not. You're an inspiration. Don't let the falconer get you down.'

'Aw.' She had a champion. 'Thank you. Music to my ears.'

'Besides, maybe you're looking at this the wrong way around. Maybe Tomas thinks he let *you* down by not preventing you from being taken in the first place. Guilt might be part of his response to you.'

'That's just stupid.'

'I speak from experience. Guilt plagues me that I did nothing to prevent your abduction. We lost *years*.'

The pain in his voice was only too real and she stopped to consider his words more carefully and form a more appropriate reply.

'If you need my forgiveness, you have it. But Cas, you were just a kid. You and Tomas were both kids. What could you possibly have done to prevent my kidnapping?'

'Something,' he muttered darkly. 'All I'm saying is that if Tomas was your unofficial secret protector, he would have guilt. I guarantee it. And our falconer doesn't particularly like being reminded that he has feelings. That's all I'm saying.'

'I'm not giving up on him.'

'What a surprise,' he replied dryly. 'I'm on your side, Claudia. I'm glad it went well today.'

'Thank you for the new perspective. I'm going to keep it in mind when I corner him next. And, brother, just so you know, I'm going to knock any harbouring of guilt for the life I've led right out of your head too.'

'Please,' he offered drolly. 'Do.'

CHAPTER THREE

CLAUDIA DECIDED TO start small when it came to desensitising Tomas to her ongoing presence in his life. She owned a falconer's training journal written in 1770 that she'd often found useful, so she had it forwarded to her and left it on his desk with a note to look at page sixty-three and see if he agreed with the method presented for treating bumblefoot. That had led to a chance encounter out by aviary three and a lively argument about the merits or otherwise of using harsh chemicals to clean perches. Tomas had argued against it, which left Claudia to take the for position.

Neither had realised how loud they'd been getting until one of the apprentices had interrupted, with every indication of having been trying to get their attention for a while.

'What about using a good old antiseptic soap, sunshine, and using a variety of perches and rotating them in and out?' he'd suggested.

There'd really been no way to argue with that. Tomas had apologised for his temper, headed for open space and refused to re-engage with her for *weeks*.

'He's not one for raising his voice,' his most senior apprentice explained when Tomas rescheduled her appointment with him yet again because of some new crisis that took him away from the fortress. 'He'll be kicking himself about the argument he got into with you last time you and he butted heads and trying to make sure it never happens again.'

Claudia stared at the older man, bewildered. 'But he didn't lose his cool. We were having a spirited intellectual debate. No falcon feet got damaged in the process.'

'He raised his voice. To him that's a failing.'

Tomas Sokolov was a big baby. A big, beautiful, unforgettable infant.

'Is there anything *I* can help you with?' the man continued.

'I want to set a date for bringing two of my falcons here permanently.'

'With due respect, ma'am, you're the Crown Princess. Pretty sure you can do that whenever you feel like it.'

'I know. But I know it'll be a stretch on resources, and he said there was an information sheet I had to fill out...' And she'd wanted to see him again... 'He wasn't really upset about that loud conversation, was he?' She refused to call it an argument.

'It's like this. Staying calm and in control is like the first commandment around here. We need it when handling the birds. We need it when conveying information respectfully and effectively to titled idiots who think they know everything about falcons when really they know nothing.'

'You mean me.'

'No, ma'am. No one here has any complaints about

the way you handle and care for the birds. But you don't know Tomas, if I may say. And he doesn't do strong emotions. He locks that sh— stuff down. Maybe he got trained to bank it down hard, you know? Maybe it's just his way. But riling him's not the way to make a connection. He won't stick around for it.'

'So you're saying it'd be a bad idea if I confessed to him that I quite liked seeing him all heated, and that I was enjoying myself. Immensely. He's very, ah—' she waved a gloved hand around in the air to explain what she meant while she searched for the right word '—compelling.'

The man couldn't quite hide his amusement. 'Right.'

'But I certainly don't want to rouse his, ah—'

'Passions,' supplied the apprentice, suspiciously dead-pan.

'Right. I wouldn't want to rouse those to the point of no return. That would be bad.'

'Nah, do it. Do him good,' said another apprentice, sticking his head out of an enclosure to join the conversation. 'Junior apprentice Bran at your service, Your Highness.'

'Hello.' So many apprentices with advice and no Tomas. 'Call me Claudia.'

'No can do, ma'am. But I'm the one in charge of the paperwork this week and if you don't mind walking with me to the office I can print out those information sheets you're after.'

'Great. And when will Tomas be returning?'

'The problem is that when he sees you flying in, he heads out,' said the ever-helpful Bran.

'Tell him he's a coward.'

Bran laughed long and loud and the older apprentice simply shook his head. 'Yeah, I don't think anyone's going to be telling the Master Falconer that.'

CHAPTER FOUR

WHEN IT CAME to hatreds, Tomas strove to be even-handed. Take capital cities swarming with people, and royal palaces swarming with courtiers, for example. Tomas happily loathed both. Not for him the niceties needed to traverse such terrain. He didn't suffer fools. He wasn't one for idle conversation. Even his conversations with Casimir bordered on brutally brief.

He was heading into the mountains tomorrow to check on the greater spotted eagle pairs, because at some point he wanted to introduce a new pair. All he had to do before he left was dress up in his royal finest and travel to the palace for an afternoon audience with his king and some kind of banquet in the evening. Didn't matter that he couldn't remember what the banquet was for, they were all the same. Get showered, get dressed, go to the capital and the palace he loathed because it was too full of random guards he didn't recognise and Claudia hadn't been safe there, and see duty done. That was the shape of his day, and he was all for getting through it efficiently.

Shower first, to wash off the stench of owl droppings and get clean again.

And then the rest.

Five minutes later he made his exit from the shower as Lor entered his quarters without knocking. She didn't usually intrude on his private space unless she felt it necessary. Like that time when a golden eagle had scored his shoulder and all down his back in a botched landing. Or when that fighting hawk had almost taken his finger off. Or like now, as she carried a pile of spruce green fabric and gold braid over one arm.

'I freshened your coat. It was dusty.'

'Thanks.' He tightened his grip on the towel that covered him from low on his hips to the start of his knees. While the trousers and shirt of his dress uniform fitted him well enough, the coat was a masterpiece fit for a coronation. It was tight fitting through the shoulders and chest and split back and front for ease of riding, but that was where practicality ended and the dust-collecting gold braid began. Embellished cuffs ran from wrist to elbow, tightened by leather buckles. He supposed a raptor could land on his forearm easily enough without damaging his skin, but the heavy gold braid embellishment didn't stop there. It formed a stiff collar around his neck, became a tight belt around his waist and dripped from the coat shoulders. It was terrible, and beautiful, and ridiculous. It was the King's Falconer's ceremonial dress. 'Do you have any idea what all this is about?'

Lor too wore her finest royal livery and her eyes, kind as they were, suggested she knew something he didn't.

'I'm afraid Lor is bound to secrecy,' said another voice from the doorway, and he sighed, because of course it was Claudia and doubtless his emotions would start acting up again.

His heels came together and he bowed his head as befitting his status and hers. Enforced formality was his last line of defence against Claudia, bane of his existence. That and speechlessness. Not that he ever seemed to stay speechless for long in her presence. His grip on his towel tightened.

'Hey.' She smiled and he didn't trust that *very* appreciative smile one little bit. 'You're running late.'

'Someone brought in an owl with a broken wing.'

'And not one of your apprentices could see to it without your supervision, hmm?'

'Exactly.'

'Nothing at all to do with you not wanting to go to the palace in the first place.'

'Nothing at all.'

That was the other problem with Claudia. She knew him too well and he didn't know *how*. He was a closed book. An impenetrable fortress. A cypher of his own making.

Who'd been blabbing about him?

'The helicopter leaves in twenty minutes,' she murmured in dulcet tones. 'The King is expecting you, me, Silas and Lor to be on it.'

'I'll be there.' She wore a royal purple travelling cloak and her long, thick hair had been wound in an elaborate crown. Her make-up was perfect. He tightened his grip on his towel, wondering if her composure would falter if he dropped it. Maybe she'd flee and give him some small reprieve from those all-seeing eyes. There was no earthly reason for her to even be in his quarters. Was there? 'Was there anything else?'

'I'll take it from here, Lor. We'll meet you at the helicopter,' Claudia said, and Lor nodded, hung the coat from a hook on his wardrobe door, and left.

Claudia stayed.

'I need to get dressed.' Chivalry demanded he give fair warning.

'What a good idea.' Claudia glanced at her delicate wristwatch that doubtless cost more than his annual wage. 'Eighteen minutes.'

Frustration bubbled. 'Leave.'

But all she did was lift an eyebrow. 'Your bathroom's right there if it's privacy you need. Your King, my brother, tasked me with getting you to the palace on time and I take my duties extremely seriously.'

He didn't need the twitch of her lips to know she was teasing. Her capacity to break rules, tradition and anything else that stood in her way was fast becoming legend.

His capacity to ignore her was rapidly becoming non-existent.

There was absolutely no ignoring this woman.

He didn't even know if he *wanted* to ignore what had been brewing between them.

With a shrug and what he hoped she took as unconcealed irritation rather than challenge accepted, he dropped his towel to the floor and strode to his chest of drawers in search of underwear. He took his time, allowed himself a flex of muscle here and a slight stretch there. His lifestyle hardly encouraged softness and his body was the result. Strongly muscled arms and shoulders gave way to a sculpted midsection that carried no fat. Long legs, strong thighs, and heavy manhood that he had every right to be proud of. He could almost feel her gaze travelling from that spot between his shoulder blades, all the way down his spine and over the globes of his buttocks. Modesty failed him in the same way propriety constantly failed her.

He half turned, noting with satisfaction the hot colour that rode her cheeks. 'What's wrong? You look a little glazed.'

'Hmm?' She dragged her gaze away from his nether regions with no small amount of effort and finally let him see the expression in her eyes. It was hot, fierce and appreciative, and his body stiffened in all the right places. 'Glazed, no. This is my so impressed I'm practically speechless face. Sixteen minutes.'

A lot could happen in sixteen minutes.

He could reach for her. Muss up those perfect lips with biting needy kisses. Bury his fingers in her hair and tilt her head just so, the better to see every tiny expression to cross her face.

Instead, he stepped into his underwear and reached for his trousers, smiling wolfishly at the regretful little sigh that reached his ears.

He reached for his shirt next and let the buttery soft ivory linen encase his arms and shoulders as if it had been made for him and not his great-grandfather. He didn't fumble the buttons at his chest, but the tiny buttons on the cuffs of the sleeves were another matter.

'Here.' She crossed the room to stand in front of him. 'Let me help.'

So he held his arm out, wrists turned up like a supplicant, as she fastened the half dozen buttons on first one cuff and then the other. He'd never been this up close and personal with her before—not as an adult. Those times when they were kids and had stretched out on the rug in front of his father's hearth as they pored over picture books of falcons didn't count. He hadn't been aware of her back then as anything but a forbidden friend who needed protection.

Her fingers were warm against his skin and her delicate touch set up a chain reaction that fizzed along his veins. She brushed her thumb over his wrist when she was done and he wondered whether it was normal for a man's pulse rate to triple beneath the act of a woman helping him put his clothes *on*.

'Coat next or boots?' she asked, and the words were plain as could be but the husky intimacy of her voice did nothing to slow his heart rate.

'Boots.' He sat on the hard wooden seat of the blanket box at the end of his bed and reached for them. Never had his room felt so small. 'Why are you here?'

'To help you prepare for your meeting with my brother. For some strange reason, he suspected an emergency might lead you elsewhere.'

She went to kneel before him and he stood abruptly and stopped her with a hand beneath her elbow. He shouldn't be touching her uninvited, but he couldn't be thinking about that now. 'Don't ever kneel before me.' He might never let her up.

'It's not weakness to honour a man so.' She held his gaze with a steady one of her own and he was the first to look away.

'Within the borders of intimacy, maybe. Not for the likes of you and me.'

'Why not you and me? You might like it.'

He definitely would like it just a little too much.

'You're sister to a king. I am my father's son. We shouldn't be doing any of this. Not the fighting. Not the flirting. Not this.' He let her go and stepped into his boots and lifted his foot up on the chest and started on the laces. 'I am but your humble servant.'

'Humble servant?' He glanced up just in time to see the ghost of a wry smile on her lips. 'Hardly. A week ago, the falcon you bred and trained for speed won the most prestigious race in four kingdoms and fifty million dollars in prize money.'

So it had.

'Your brother's bird, your brother's money.'

'And *your* win. Your face as it happened was as proud and fierce as any king's.'

'You should have been watching the falcon.'

'And miss seeing you in action? I'm not that stupid. As for my royal blood being a barrier to any future association between us, my blood may not be as blue as you think. My so-called father believed my mother slept with his brother and had decided I was no child of his long before I was born. A cuckoo in his nest, so to speak.'

Tomas couldn't hide his shock. He'd never heard such rumours—and he would have if they'd ever been circulated. 'Who told you that?'

'Cas.'

He didn't want to believe any of it. And yet…

'Explains a lot, doesn't it,' Claudia continued. 'My mother took her own life—can't ask her. Cas believes his father murdered my father. Fratricide, they call it. All of them taking their secrets to the grave. Cas doesn't care who sired me so long as I stand by his side as his sister, serve as a bridge between Byzenmaach and the north, and keep our family secrets secret.'

'Then why tell me? Why not do as your king commands and *hold your tongue*?'

'Because before we reach the palace, I want you to believe beyond doubt that I'm in no way bound by titles and blood status. You could have befriended me at any time these past months. You must know I crave your company.'

'I know you *think* you do. I still haven't figured out why.'

'Look to your character. I like it. Hell, look in a mirror. Think about what happens whenever we touch.'

'Nothing happens.'

'Speak for yourself. I get shivers.'

'Nothing happens.'

'Imagine what would happen if we ever had sex. If you say nothing happens I'm going to revert to toddlerhood and pull your hair.'

He smirked. He couldn't help it.

'Are you ever going to put more clothes on, or am I just going to stand here and pant?' She slipped his coat from its hanger and held it out. The coat obscured her face but the impatient shake she gave it spoke volumes.

'I'm about to be presented with a new title and home. I don't know if I'm excited about it or not. Lor and Silas are getting stuff too. You're being honoured for winning that falcon race. I can't believe you haven't guessed that last bit already. Thirteen minutes. Hurry up.'

Moved to action, he thrust his arms into the sleeves and shrugged into the ceremonial coat. He stayed absolutely still as she fussed with the positioning of the shoulders and brushed her hand across his broad back.

'Hmm,' she murmured.

'What now?'

'Tight fit.'

He knew that. 'It'll be worse when the buttons are done up, so I'll leave them loose until we get to the capital.' He'd done this before, he knew how to stay as comfortable as possible for as long as possible.

'What about the buckles on the sleeves?'

'They can be done now.' He turned and caught a waft of faint fragrance, something velvety and rich. 'Is that why Leonidas refused your return after the kidnapping? Because you weren't his?' It took a while, what with all her talk of craving him, but his brain did eventually kick in around their earlier conversation thread.

'Probably.' She reached for the first buckle, her fingers quick and nimble. 'They'd have had better luck taking Cas. Instead, they snatched a second-born girl child and likely not even his. Little wonder the King reacted as he did.'

'And yet your captors let you live.'

'I know plenty of my political opponents think I've got Stockholm Syndrome, but my captors were not bad people. Misguided, yes. Naïve to think they'd just be able to hand me back and take a seat at the negotiating table—Leonidas would have been perfectly capable of sitting them down and slaughtering them, don't you think?'

'Well, I do *now*.'

'But my captors weren't child killers. They didn't cut off any of my body parts and send them back in the post. In many ways they were very kind to me. They reminded me of you and your father.'

He was aghast. 'Is that supposed to be a *compliment*?'

'Clearly you don't think so.'

He could do nothing but stare.

'I had my very own pony, wolfhound and falcon, and substitute parents who treated me far better than my own ever had. I had other children all around me and a nomadic lifestyle that made every day an adventure. I begged them to keep me. Promised I'd be useful to them one day.'

He didn't like her captors and never would. He would sooner gut Lord Ildris, her advisor, than look at him, and the other man knew it. They claimed ground around each other very, very carefully.

'They took you as an act of ill intent. Ripped you from your home because they wanted more for themselves.' Tomas *didn't* forgive them their sins.

She'd finished with the buckles on one vambrace. He lowered his arm and raised the other. 'Did you ever think of the people you left behind? The ones who grieved for you and thought of you and blamed themselves for years because they couldn't keep you safe?'

As soon as the words left his mouth, he knew he'd revealed too much. He might as well have screamed *What about me?* Her fingers faltered, clumsy, and then she found the strap again and pulled the buckle way too tight. 'Easy,' he muttered.

'Sorry.' She loosened it and found the right buckle hole.

'The apology is mine,' he offered gruffly. 'What you did to survive, how you coped after being taken, is none of my business. I'm glad your captors realised your worth and treated you kindly. I reserve the right to question their humanity.'

She dropped her gaze to his vambrace, long lashes shielding her expression. 'I missed Cas terribly at first. Then I decided he'd take far fewer beatings if I wasn't around because he wouldn't have to protect me. I decided I was protecting him for once. I was a hero in my own imagination.' She finished doing up the buckles and he let his hand drop as she looked up at him through her lashes, her eyes glittering with tears. 'I missed you and your father and the falcons most of all. I knew you'd be worried and that you'd…grieve…if you thought me dead.'

'I prayed for you,' he confessed gruffly. He'd hidden himself away in places no one could find him and prayed as hard as he could for her safe return. 'I grieved.'

She'd held a special place in his heart for so many years. Beloved. Untouchable.

Dead.

And yet here she was, spinning him round, twisting him inside out, because he didn't know what to *feel* when he was in her presence.

'I'm sorry.' She was going to ruin her make-up if she let those tears fall. 'All I wanted was to feel safe. And loved. Both. That's still my guiding star and something I seek again as an adult. In a lover.'

There was too much honesty in this conversation for him to reply.

He shrugged away from her instead. Heaven, give him space.

'I called my first pony Tomas. My first wolfhound Tom-Tom. My first falcon Toot Lolo,' she told him and then took a step back. 'Call me obsessed. I won't deny it. I wanted to remember you any way I could.' Delicate colour stained her cheeks as she tugged the sleeve of her travelling cloak aside to glance at her wristwatch again. 'Three minutes,' she said, as if she could force briskness upon them. 'You might want to do something with your hair. It's sticking up all over the place.'

He retreated to the bathroom, feeling flayed around the edges. Heartsore over the naming of a bird. He normally took a towel to his hair then ran his fingers through it for good measure, but he was six weeks past due for a haircut and maybe this time he could use a comb.

Maybe doing something so menial would bury the urge to take his fingers to her hair and mess it up beyond redemption as he pressed slow kisses to her cheeks and her eyes and inevitably her mouth.

He met his own gaze in the mirror and narrowed his

eyes and flattened his mouth until he looked fierce and forbidding, all other emotions forcefully contained.

Better.

She smiled when he exited the bathroom and he scowled his reply, but did that deter her?

'You look amazing,' she murmured approvingly. 'I'm grateful you're not yet married or otherwise attached. Why is that? Lack of opportunity? Hidden vice? A solitary nature?'

'I am what I am.' It wasn't his fault he'd never yet found a woman who could handle him in the long term. 'Don't analyse me.'

'You're asking the impossible.'

'You've risen from the dead once already.' As far as he was concerned, she was mistress of the impossible. 'Just do it.'

Claudia waited impatiently as her brother's equerry stood by the closed double doors to the throne room and ticked her, Tomas, Silas and Lor off the guest list. It was an honours day with Cas in residence, intent on bestowing riches on the worthy. Silas and Lor—being well past retirement age—were being gifted a grace-and-favour cottage within the walls of the winter fortress and a generous stipend to replace their wages. If they weren't yet ready to retire, there was now a plan in place for them to step back gradually from their vast responsibilities. Silas's bones had been brittle of late. It was time to slow down.

Claudia was being gifted a previously mothballed duchy on Byzenmaach's northernmost border, and it encompassed the winter fortress in its entirety. Henceforth, she would be known as Princess Claudia, the Princess Royal, King's Counsel and Duchess of Ayerlon. So many daunting titles and she vowed to do them all justice.

As for Tomas, he too would receive his due.

She'd had a hand in it, of course. All he had to do was keep an open mind.

The King was waiting for them just inside the doors and Tomas entered and bowed as he was introduced by name and lineage. His family had been falcon masters for centuries and in service to the King for the last three generations, and he was proud of that legacy. He knew he would have to take a wife soon to secure the family name, but he was still in his early thirties. There was still time to find someone suitable.

Don't go there, he told himself fiercely. Do *not* picture Claudia of Byzenmaach in your bed.

He who'd spent years honing his senses so he would always be in control of his reactions and his raptors had a dominant streak a mile wide in the bedroom. He *liked* being in control. It was a point of pride that he could just as easily satisfy his partners with soft, slow kisses and attentiveness as he could when he got his edge on. The point was, he *never* lost his head. He never stopped noticing and analysing everything about the person he was with.

He did not want to think about what might happen if he added Claudia and a mountain of unresolved feelings to *that* mix.

He stood in line, waiting his turn to stand before his

King, and tried not to look too shocked when Claudia—regal and resplendent in a rose-coloured ballgown and diamond choker and earrings—received a duchy that encompassed the finest mountain wilderness in all the land. It included the winter fortress. That fortress so casually traded was his *home*, and indignation prickled at his skin, already held tight by the fine fabric of a coat that had been made for ceremony rather than for him.

He watched, silently seething but outwardly a picture of calm, as her brother held out his hand and she took it and rose and kissed him on each cheek before moving on.

Silas and Lor then took her place in front of Casimir and Tomas wondered, not for the first time, how old they were. Were they in their eighties already? Late seventies? They'd been old when he was a kid. Kind and patient with him, the grandparents of his heart in lieu of blood kin.

Tomas listened as Silas and Lor were given a pathway towards living out their days in a manner both generous and respectful of the many years they'd called the winter fortress home. It was fitting, and Tomas grudgingly approved.

And then it was his turn and he wondered exactly what Casimir had in mind for him.

He was too young to retire, so why was he here?

'Tomas Sokolov, son of Andreas, grandson of Yos,' King Casimir began. 'Your skill and dedication to the sport of falconry has brought Byzenmaach great standing. Your breeding programmes for endangered species are acknowledged worldwide. My sister vouches for your kindness and protective nature when we were children. My wife and daughter cherish your patience and gentleness with them. Beyond that, I know you, Master Falconer. I see your dedication to the welfare of all in your care and your passion for your causes. It's time to spread your wings.'

'Are you firing me?' Because he couldn't. *Surely* he wouldn't? Tomas had been nothing but loyal, and although he had apprentices to pass his knowledge on to, it would take years before any of the current crop could replace him. 'Fair warning, many of the birds in my care will go where I go.' It wasn't an idle threat. 'There's no other way.' Casimir *knew* this, surely. 'They're imprinted on me.'

'Good thing I'm rewarding you rather than letting you go, then, isn't it.' Casimir sounded exasperated. 'Happy surprise, my arse. I knew I should have warned you in advance.'

Tomas held his tongue as Equerry Dorn approached with a weathered scroll sitting atop a velvet pillow. Claudia held a similar scroll in her now gloved hand.

'Kneel.'

Tomas held his tongue some more, bowed his head and knelt before his King.

'Tomas Sokolov, I bequeath to you the Barony of Aergoveny, henceforth to be held by you and your descendants, male or female, for as long as your bloodline exists. The land is mountainous, with summer grazing in the high passes. There's a village with several families in residence within your borders and they pay pennies in local government taxes in return for being left largely to themselves. I'm reliably informed that several people there have expressed interest in becoming apprenticed to you, should you want to encourage it.'

'I already have apprentices,' he murmured beneath his breath.

'Have some more. A modest manor house surrounded by solid outer walls lies east of the village—I have stonemasons working to bring it back in good repair. There are aviaries, stables and animal enclosures that should please you. As for funds, which you're going to need, I bestow upon you the prize money recently won by the falcon Sweetybird McTender Heart, otherwise known as Cloud—we seriously need to work on those bird names, Master Falconer, if we're going to keep winning major competitions.'

'Blame your daughter.' Tomas sneaked a glance at the other man, unsure if this was some kind of elaborate joke, or maybe just a dream. But he'd never dreamed of being an aristocrat—and it wasn't because he lacked ambition. He ran one of the most ambitious endangered raptor breed-and-release programmes in Europe. But he emphatically didn't want the responsibility to *people* that came with an aristocrat's title, and he'd make a terrible Lord. Could he refuse the honour? Maybe not publicly, maybe not now, but later?

Did he *want* to refuse fifty million dollars?

Casimir's eyes narrowed and Tomas swiftly bowed his head.

'In addition to the prize money, as per the competition rules of 1649, I grant you permission to keep *two* wives, now that you have the monetary means to do so.'

What?

'Rules are rules.'

Tomas felt the tap of a ceremonial sword on each shoulder. This wasn't real. It couldn't be. He was no nobleman. He barely had table manners. But Casimir was smiling and taking a scroll from a purple velvet pillow and handing it to him and people were applauding, so maybe it wasn't a dream after all.

'Arise Lord Sokolov, King's Falconer, Baron of Aergoveny. Welcome to the circus.'

CHAPTER FIVE

H E WASN'T TAKING it well. Claudia scoured the banquet hall that heaved with all the people and the families of the people who had received honours that day. Tomas stood alone, silent and forbidding. There'd been no Sokolov family to invite—his parents and grandparents were dead and, according to Silas and Lor, who'd acted as his surrogate family for years, he had no extended family.

The way he stood with his feet slightly apart and his arms behind his back suggested a man perfectly at ease. The tension in that perfectly chiselled jaw and the ice in his eyes for anyone he didn't know suggested otherwise. The look he'd given her a few minutes earlier had been glacial enough to compete with the highest mountain peaks. She'd raised her chin and offered her most challenging smile in return.

Your move, my lord.

Sadly, he'd yet to move an inch.

'You're glaring,' said a voice from beside her and she turned to survey her brother, resplendent in ceremonial garb. 'Little wrinkles around your eyes, here and here.' Cas touched his own face in ever helpful fashion. 'Why are you glaring?'

As if he didn't know. 'Two. Wives.'

Cas smirked. 'Don't look at me. The right to two wives came with the prize money. Of course, the rules go on to say that should a man's first wife object to the taking of a second one, the first wife gets the inflationary indexed equivalent of all the prize money. She can do whatever she wants with it.'

Claudia contemplated this latest bit of information. 'How perfectly brutal.'

'I knew you'd like it.' He touched the space between his eyebrows. 'Still with the little wrinkles.'

'I don't like these events.'

'Who does? And yet they serve a valuable purpose. Who should praise and encourage good deeds and excellence if not a country's leader?' Her brother's smile cooled. 'You were the one who came back, Claudia. To advocate for change, you said. To be of use. Well, the price to pay is your presence in my inner circle and that means a million more banquets like this one. You know this.'

She did know.

She'd made that devil's bargain. She had her brother's ear. He *listened* when she spoke of the concerns and needs of those who straddled the borders to the north. More than that, he'd offered consultation and collaboration and respect for a nomadic way of life he couldn't possibly understand because he'd never lived it.

But she had lived that life of freedom, throughout her childhood, teens and early adulthood, and sometimes she missed it so much she wanted to weep and rage at the loss of it.

Now was one of those times.

She'd lobbied hard for Tomas to be given the barony and the prize money. He needed more room for more birds and the ability to expand his activities in that arena as he saw fit. He could be so much more than just a king's falconer, and Casimir needed strong, steadfast noblemen who could help preserve the mountain regions.

She hadn't realised until this moment, watching Tomas glower at her from across the room, that he might not have wanted to trade freedom for riches.

'It's going to work,' she murmured, suddenly desperate for reassurance. 'It has to.'

Cas stared and she lifted her chin high, even as fierce heat flooded her cheeks. She didn't usually display her vulnerability, at least not in public. She was the stolen princess who'd returned to her country, fierce and unbroken, some twenty years later. She had a myth to uphold. Desperately wanting approval for her actions didn't fit her image at all.

'Don't stare,' she told her brother. 'It's impolite.'

'I'm so sorry.' The tenderness in his voice slid through all the cracks in her armour and she silently cursed him for it. 'I didn't realise your feelings for our falconer ran so deep.'

'Well, now you know, and I'll thank you to keep your newfound insight to yourself. Tomas is going to love Aergoveny when he sees it. He'll be his own man, free to live and love as he pleases, and maybe he'll live well and choose to love me. That's my big master plan. Lame, isn't it.'

'It has a few holes in it, Cas conceded. 'You do realise that being pushy might not get you what you want?'

'Well, that's going to be annoying.'

Cas snorted. 'Poor Tomas.'

'Not any more.' She fixed Cas with her sternest gaze.
'You *are* getting ready to leave so we can all get out of
here, right?' No one could leave before Cas made his
exit. 'Rudolpho's been eyeing his watch and giving you
stern glances for at least fifteen minutes.'

Rudolpho was Cas's valet or equerry or private secretary—it depended on requirements. Rudolpho kept her
brother's days doable.

Cas nodded but made no move to leave. 'If I may be
so bold as to make a suggestion concerning our new-
est baron?'

'You may. Provided it's *only* a suggestion.' One she
could ignore.

Cas rolled his eyes and then leaned over to whisper
words for her ears only.

'*Patience, sister.*'

Claudia had five minutes, if that, once Casimir took
his leave before others started leaving too. So while
Cas headed towards Rudolpho, Claudia made a beeline
for Tomas.

'I have the keys to the map room,' she said as soon as
she reached his side. 'Would you like to see drawings
of the lands now under your care?'

'This is your doing.' The repressed fury in his voice
gave her pause. She'd never seen Tomas properly angry.
He was a man of infinite patience when it came to his

birds, and horses and wolfhounds. Any beast, really. Even their occasional, ahem, arguments, hadn't involved full fury. Until now. '*You* put this *reward* in your brother's ear.'

The way he said the word *reward* made it perfectly clear he thought of it as something else entirely.

'Cas didn't need any convincing—if that's your problem.'

'I don't want a barony and great piles of money. I don't need them. I have enough responsibility.'

'To your birds.'

'Exactly. I don't need any responsibility to people. I don't generally *like* people.'

'Is that really true, though?' She nodded and smiled at her brother across the room as he finally took his leave. Tomas noticed, he always had been observant, and sketched a brief bow of his own towards the retreating monarch. 'Because you get on well enough with Silas and Lor. And Ana and Sophia and the stable master and his family and your apprentices.' There were others she could name. 'And they like you. You're firm and fair and I hear tell you have a kind heart.'

For those who could find it.

'Maybe what you don't like is thinking that you're going to somehow let people down, but I don't think you will.'

His scowl had intensified and she redoubled her efforts to convince him that she'd done the right thing for everyone concerned.

'The people of Aergoveny have been ignored for a very long time and they've heard of you, Tomas. They want their high country preserved, and who better to do that than a baron in need of vast tracts of wilderness, into which he can release all manner of wild creatures? They're willing to show a lot of respect to a man who can honour them and their children and preserve the old ways of falconry. They're already tuned to protecting habitat, as are you. As am I. You're going to be an excellent fit, and I, as mistress of the winter fortress, am going to support you in every way I can.'

Did he really not understand what she was trying to do?

'Aergoveny is yours now. And it's a big change from what you're used to, but think of what you can achieve. You can appoint a steward to help with the day-to-day management of your household and the surrounding lands. You can employ people to help you accomplish goals. You know how important remote settlements can be for those who inhabit them. You know how they run.'

His silence unsettled her.

'You can expand your breeding programmes, take on seasonal apprentices, invite experts from all over the world to stay under your roof. Hatch plans that reflect your values and no one can stop you now. It's freedom.'

'It's a cage.'

'You've been bound since birth by your family's service to the Crown. That's a cage too. This cage is bigger,' she snapped.

Patience, sister.

So much for sound advice.

She focused on her breathing, slowed it down, and tried not to push too hard and too fast.

All he had to do was give his new life a chance. Give *her* a chance. She was a woman of great confidence and clarity—everyone said so, and most of the time it was true.

She wouldn't disappoint.

'And, in addition, presenting you with the means to excel even more in your chosen field, as a nobleman, you and I are now on a far more level playing field.' And if he still didn't get it, 'Meaning that if you want to, you're now well placed to pursue me. Romantically. *Openly.*' Because that was important too.

Had she really imagined the fire in his eyes all those times he'd looked at her before turning resolutely away? Had she misjudged the way he watched her when he thought no one was looking? Had he been unable to keep his eyes off her because she dazzled him or had he simply been keeping watch to make sure she wasn't spirited away again by forces unknown?

'I'm not written into your future. I wouldn't do that,' she assured him. 'But I am a possibility. I always have been. I've just made things a bit easier for us, should you ever actually want me.'

He was like a big, silent wall. The resplendent King's Falconer, with his iron will and magnificent body and eyes of deepest brown.

'It goes against my nature having someone else call the shots *the way you so very clearly do,*' he said finally.

Was that meant to be a warning?

'You like being in control, yes, yes, I know. Probably in the bedroom too, am I right? I've heard rumours of your, um, prowess. I am here for you in that regard. I know what I like and I definitely like that. You be you. I'll be me. I'm very fond of saying please.'

More silence greeted her earnest words. Startled, bemused silence, dripping incredulity all over the marble floor.

'So would you like to see the map room now or would you rather take another decade or two to think about it?'

She'd had such good plans for them this evening. Was it too much to ask for a thimbleful of cooperation?

'I'm going home.'

She could work with that. Privacy was all they needed.

'I'm getting out of these stupid clothes.'

Yes, yes, exactly!

'And then I'm going to do what I planned to do all along, and take a trip into the mountains for a couple of weeks and do my job, and fulfil the commitments I made before you so helpfully rearranged my *world*.'

He had no idea how badly she wanted to pull on her travelling furs and ride out there with him. The problem with that plan being that she had political commitments all next week, along with two royal luncheons and a trip to a neighbouring kingdom as her brother's envoy.

'If you can postpone your trip for a week, I could come with you.'

'No.'

'You are *so* infuriating.'

'Me? You think I'm the infuriating one in this—' he made a sharp gesture with his arm as if he couldn't find the right word '—this...'

'Relationship?' she supplied hopefully.

'Conversation! That's all this is. A conversation.'

'I'm disappointed in you. At least call it a battle of wits.'

'No.'

'Robust courting?'

'Wrong again. You made me a lord. On a *whim*.'

'It wasn't a whim. It was a carefully considered reward for your service to falconry, a savvy political move on Cas's part, and an act of utmost faith in your character.'

He stared at her for what seemed like an eternity.

'And I'm not giving up on you.' Might as well get that out in the open too.

'Oh, for the—

'For the what?'

At least he was talking again.

'Show me the blasted map room!'

He wasn't capitulating. Just because he was walking down a long, empty corridor in a section of the palace he'd never been in before, with the terror that was Claudia leading the way, didn't mean that he thought any of this was right and good, or that he deserved to be called anyone's lord.

He was doing this because public showdowns had never been his style and he and Claudia had been heading straight for one.

He was following her lead because he'd needed to get away from prying eyes and fawning courtiers and she'd offered him a way to do so that afforded him minimal contact with others.

That was what he told himself and he mostly believed it.

Right up until they entered the map room with its vaulted ceilings and wooden tables and feature lamps illuminating priceless parchment. A fire crackled merrily in the enormous stone hearth, and supper had been laid out on a sideboard.

Claudia smiled her approval and let out a little sigh as if she too had found the ceremonial events taxing. 'Make yourself at home,' she said, and proceeded to remove one earring and then its pair. 'You have no idea how heavy old jewellery is. It was my mother's and I'm supposed to have some sort of mystical emotional connection to it, but I don't. It feels like a noose.' Her hands went to the clasp of her necklace and she moved closer and turned her back on him. 'Would you mind? There's a clasp disguised as a flower with a little pearl in the middle and you have to push on the pearl and then—oh, okay, you've done this before.' The clasp came apart and she caught the necklace before it could fall. 'Thanks.'

The fact that she looked so put-out by his apparent expertise put him in a better mood than he'd been in all day. He didn't bother to say 'No problem', figuring his smirk spoke for him.

Non-verbal cues were his strength, after all.

She slid him a sideways glance as she placed the jewels on a nearby table and started tugging on her gloves, one fabric finger at a time until she'd taken those off too.

'Feel free to take off your coat,' she murmured, knowing full well that he couldn't do so without her help.

'I won't be here long enough to settle in.'

She made that small hmm she was so fond of. The one that never failed to make his manhood stand up and take notice. 'There are ledgers here too. Stocking rates and harvest figures courtesy of the last Baron of Aergoveny back in 1672. Are you sure you don't want to at least undo all those buttons on your coat?'

'Positive.' He was one hundred percent sure she was downright evil, knowing as she did that he'd left doing those buttons up until the last possible minute. But he needed to be in control of something, even something as insignificant as when he undressed. 'You're bossy.'

'I prefer to call it having leadership skills.' Now she was the one with the smirk, and it was infuriating.

'Not quite the same thing.'

'Hmm.' She headed for one of the far tables and turned on a lamp to illuminate the map placed upon it. It had the ripples that came of being rolled up for a long time, and someone had placed strips of lead around the edges to keep it flat. He wanted to remain unmoved, but the weight of history and continuity wore him down. Even so...

'How can this be owned by anyone?'

'It can't,' she said simply. 'We just pretend. But you can be a steward, with protection your goal.'

'I never asked for this.'

She traced the outline of the estate with her forefinger. 'The land suits your needs perfectly. It may not seem like home to you at first, but as the years pass, surely that will change. Your Barony could become one of the greatest reserves in northern Byzenmaach and beyond. Cas is already pressuring neighbouring kings to dedicate land in that mountain range to preservation. You can lead conversation and influence policy and all you have to do is believe.' She turned to face him, her eyes beseeching. 'Protection for this land. Financial independence and opportunity for you and yours. Why can't you see this as an opportunity? Is it because I'm the one who fought for it?'

The things he wanted to *do* to her.

'My hands are rough. *I* can be rough. My sexual appetite is strong. Coarse. Greedy.' So he'd been told. 'I'm not a nobleman.'

Her eyes glowed.

'Claudia, it's a *warning*.' He couldn't be more plain. 'I would ruin you if I let desire rule me. Rule *us*.'

'Please try. You have my full permission. Because I certainly want to ruin you. I'd even put you back together afterwards. You have my word.'

'You are so—'

She stopped his words with her lips against his and as far as tactics went it was ridiculously effective.

His coat was too tight and her lips were too warm. The skin of her cheek was softer than feathers against his calloused fingers. She was finer than any woman he'd ever kissed and his mad, hidden desire for her made itself well and truly evident. She was a gossamer butterfly beneath his hands and he still had control—a slender silken thread of it. He hadn't ruined anything yet.

Only after her eyelashes fluttered closed did he slip his leash enough to savour her, tilting his head for better access and taking his fill. He fitted her body to his so easily, or maybe he gathered her in—was he holding her too tightly?—hard to know his own strength, and he felt honoured, and hounded and completely adrift from reality in this room of maps and traps and other people's history. He didn't know who he was any more or where he fitted in the grand schemes of kings, but he knew without doubt that if he could kiss like this every day he would be a wealthy man.

And for every bit of common sense that said no, Tomas, back up a bit and *think*, desire made him stupid.

He didn't stop her when she unbuttoned his coat and the shirt beneath it too, because he wanted her hands on his skin so badly, and she seemed intent on delivering. When her nails scraped lightly across his skin and edged across his nipple with a quick and sudden change in pressure, digging in like a claw, he shuddered his approval. When her lips left his to trail across to his jaw, pillow-soft right up until that moment when she nipped the sensitive skin just behind his ear, he groaned. New kink. Formerly unknown hotspot.

'Do that again.'

And she laughed against his skin and soothed with her tongue, catching his earlobe and, hello. He wouldn't object to her spending more time there too, but right now her kisses were more important. He could lose himself if he wasn't careful.

And right now, he definitely wasn't being careful.

When he lowered the zip at the side of her gown, a hidden item he'd spent some time looking for in the ballroom when fantasising about undressing her, his only thought was *yes*. He could be gentle, and the smooth slide of haute-couture undoings proved it.

See?

She was beautiful in the lamplight, all golden skin and rosy flushes, and he bent his head to her breast and drew a cry of pleasure that would stay with him for ever.

She was generous in her praise of his every move. So willing to go where he led. That he wanted to savour every moment, and she wanted to rush, made her huff and him laugh. Slowly, he unwound for her and let the fire between them burn hot and needy.

When his fingers dipped beneath her panties, she swiftly got rid of them and stood before him, naked but for her glittering pearl-coloured stilettos, as she placed the palm of her hand over his manhood and claimed his mouth with kisses that grew wilder with every breath.

There was a tabletop *right there*, and she scored his back with her polished nails as he shoved his trousers out of the way, lifted her up and dragged her against him so she was barely resting on the table edge and the rest of her rested on *him*. She closed her thighs and legs around him, cradled him, and it only took a moment to lift her up and on, and his forehead connected with hers as she whimpered and they both looked as, inch by inch, she took him in.

He'd never felt anything like it—this haunting, perfect homecoming.

She gasped, or was it a whimper, as he clenched his teeth and clutched the hard edge of the table rather than leave bruises on *her*, as he fought to stay in control so that he didn't drive too deep, but her whispered words weren't exactly helping, broken curses smattered with '*yes*' and '*don't stop*' and '*more*'.

'Lie back,' he muttered harshly, hoping to make their joining more comfortable for her. 'Let me.'

Let him put his calloused thumb to her centre and press it against his thick ridge as he tried so hard to be gentle with her and limit the power of his thrusts. Let him raise her arms above her head and clasp her wrists together as he teased and suckled her areolas to pointed nubbins.

Let me lose my way in the slap of flesh against flesh and hope you like rough edges.

Watch you twist and brace as I steal whimpers straight from your mouth, and I warned you it would be like this.

Heaven was opening up before him, warm and slick, and, no matter how hard he tried to be otherwise, Tomas was not a gentleman.

Claudia had relatively modest expectations for the concept of heaven on earth, right up until the moment Tomas entered her and unleashed his emotions. His earthy, uninhibited desire flat-out worked for her—so much for his muttered words of warning—and he was beautiful in the lamplight. A golden-skinned warrior, finally hers to hold. A hard man, barely able to contain his fascination for her softest places because he had none of his own. He was like an aphrodisiac made especially for her, and she was rushing towards a finish line that was far too close, because once she crossed it the pleasure might stop.

'No,' she whispered when he repositioned them both so he could put a thumb to her centre. She clutched at his wrist and felt him freeze. 'I'm not going to last.' She guided his hand north and pressed a kiss to his knuckles.

He smiled then, and all but melted her with its sweetness. 'You can go again.' But this time when he began to move, his hips were slow and sure, with a sensuous roll and drag guaranteed to send her into orbit anyway. 'Better?'

She closed her eyes on a particularly close brush with the end. 'Not exactly going to fix my problem.'

'How sad,' he murmured into the skin of her neck, and did it again, and again, as she arched up into him, chasing whatever wild magic he was delivering. There was no going back now—only up, up.

And over.

'Bastard.' It had to be said.

Tomas found his completion moments after Claudia left earth, and she laughed, because it was all so glittering bright and perfect.

His hair clung to his forehead in damp curls. Her princess bun likely resembled a bird's nest. She pressed a kiss to his temple as his ragged breathing slowed and so did hers. Their bodies were so in sync. She laughed again, inviting him to share her joy. 'Whatever will we do for an encore?'

Tomas said nothing, and she re-entered the earth's orbit with a searing sense of disappointment. Their bodies hadn't lied but minds lied all the time. Memories lied. Self-evaluation was notoriously unreliable.

'Don't say anything awful,' she begged.

'You'll bruise.' She could barely hear the words within his gravelly rumble.

She could work with that. 'My lover's desire mapped out on my skin. A compliment.'

'Don't humour me.'

'There's no shame in honest desire. My marks will be on you too. I want you to regret their fading.'

He drew a ragged breath.

'I want this.' Could she be any more direct? 'I want to be with you like this again. Don't pack all that fierce, gorgeous emotion away. There's nothing wrong with it. I don't bring out the worst in you, do I? Because, from where I stand, this is the very best of you and I am here for it. Why can't we see where this attraction ends?'

'You're a myth.' He loosened his hold and stepped away and moments later she was sitting naked on the table while he tugged his trousers into place.

'And you're not?' She began to laugh, harder this time, and wondered whether he'd still be here when laughter turned to tears. She'd known that rushed intimacy might deliver a rough landing, and that she would feel fragile in the face of his withdrawal. She'd taken that risk anyway. 'You've been my rescuer since I was seven years old. For real to begin with, and then in my dreams. But I'm prepared to consider you a real person—complex and flawed—if you'll do the same for me.'

'I'm no rescuer,' he said, and the tight fury in his voice made her stop and listen, even though she'd scooped up her dress and the best thing to do would be to put it on rather than strangle it with her bare hands. 'I wanted to find you and keep you safe but, no matter where I looked, you weren't there. I failed you.'

'No! You saved me from so many beatings. You spoke

up for me and persuaded your father to take me under his wing and gave me a getaway place and moments to look forward to. Once they took me, I didn't really expect you to—' *Save me.* But she had expected that, and maybe deep down she *still* expected him to make life here in Byzenmaach more bearable. 'I knew you wouldn't come for me. How could you?'

And yet how many nights had she stayed awake *hoping* he'd crawl into her tent, hold out his hand and whisk her to safety? Especially in those early days. Maybe Tomas wasn't the only one who needed to deal with the past and admit *all* the emotions. Even the ugly ones.

'I mean, I could dream, but you were just a boy and I *knew* there was nothing you could do. You were powerless, like me.'

'Is this conversation meant to make me feel *better*?' He'd half turned to stare at her from beneath a lowered brow and he was every bit as forbidding as the apex predators he served.

'I'm rather hoping it's not going to send you straight to therapy,' she muttered, slipping the gown over her head. 'Who cares if I'm a fantasy princess to you and you're a Galahad figure to me? We can work with that. Neither of us is powerless *now*. We *have* control of our lives going forward. We're outstanding together in bed, even if our communication elsewhere still needs work. And I for one have worked my arse off to get to this moment and I'm exhilarated.'

By the time she'd wrestled the gown in place, he had the buttons on his shirt done up and was helping himself to a glass of water over by the sideboard. He poured one for her too, but didn't bring it over.

'So, can I pencil you in for a private dinner and dessert some time soon?' she asked. 'After you return from your trip into the mountains?'

'You're relentless.'

'Is that a yes?'

He shrugged and drew attention to those stunningly broad shoulders, and she tried not to let her eyes glaze over with renewed sexual appreciation. Probably too soon. But he noticed her reaction, and was that a slight shoulder muscle flex just for her? Maybe there was hope for them yet.

'I'll be away for at least three weeks.'

She'd waited longer for less. 'Okay.'

'I might swing by Aergoveny on my way back.'

'You should.'

He nodded, still with his back to her, and then gestured awkwardly towards the array of bottles on the sideboard. 'May I pour you something stronger?'

'I'll have the Highland single malt Scotch, please. No ice.'

'There's ice?'

'In the silver ice bucket with the lid.'

'How *anyone* thought I'd make a decent aristocrat…'

'You will.' He had a generous and deft hand when pouring, a certain grace about him as he crossed the room and handed it to her. 'You could join me in a drink.'

A tentative knock on the library door diverted his attention. Alarm flashed in his eyes as he looked at her. 'What is it?' he barked, every word forbidding.

The door stayed closed. 'A messenger from King Casimir, Lord Aergoveny. He says to tell you the helicopter is leaving for the winter fortress at ten p.m.'

'I'll be on it.'

Claudia glanced at her watch. Twenty minutes from now. So much for persuading him to stay the night with her.

'Your brother's protecting your reputation,' said Tomas with a frown, once the sound of footsteps had retreated.

'Or yours,' she pointed out. 'Possibly his. Likely all three. You don't need the added complication of being known as my lover while establishing your new position. Cas doesn't need people thinking him a soft king who would bestow a barony on you at my request—not that he *did*.' Basic statecraft. She *knew* this. *Patience, Claudia.* 'He's looking out for us.'

'You mean he's controlling the situation because we've failed to do so.'

'Nonsense. We've got this.'

'Princess…'

They were back to honorifics and her heart broke a little because she'd thought they were done with that.

'Don't Princess me.'

'Today has been…a lot,' he continued, without uttering her name. 'And while I'm ambitious in my own way, I've never sought a barony. I've never thought about what that could mean. I've never imagined this, us, being something that could happen openly, and I need time to think about that too.'

'Unbridled passion not about to sway you?'

He huffed a reluctant laugh. 'Clearly it *did*.'

'I want…' Did it even matter what she wanted in the face of his retreat? 'My brother warned me about being pushy. I should have listened to him.' *Patience, Claudia*. Let the man catch up. 'To your freedom, Tomas. To happiness and fulfilment, no matter where your road leads. My hearth is ever open to you and yours.' She set her drink down and pressed her hands to her chest and then extended them towards him, one cupped hand sitting atop the other to form a heart shape. It was a formal farewell offered by the people of the high north. A pledge of unconditional support, no matter what the future might bring. 'Safe travels, Master Falconer, Lord Sokolov of Aergoveny.'

He brought his heels together and bowed his head. 'Thank you. I'll…be in touch.'

She hated slippery words and empty promises. Especially from a man who'd already pleaded his need for space. 'Break my heart now and quickly if you must. I hate false hope.'

'Isn't that all I've ever given you?' He was back to being harsh and distant.

'Why would you even think that?' If he didn't leave soon, hot tears would fall. 'No,' she said earnestly. 'You gave me reason to hope. Nothing false about it. Just like there's nothing false about what I'm offering. But if you don't want it, go. Leave me some dignity.' As much as could be gathered with her lopsided hair and sated body and heart he had no desire to claim.

'I'll be away for three weeks, maybe more. Will you be at the fortress when I return?'

Her fortress now. Also the only home he'd ever known. Awkward. But then, she'd left so many places in her lifetime, even special ones. If Aergoveny didn't work out for him and he wanted to return to the winter fortress, she would move on. She could occupy the rooms set aside for her here at the palace. She could build something. 'I return there on the eighteenth. And you have another helicopter to catch in…eleven minutes. Time to go, Lord Sokolov.' See? She could do stilted formality too.

He ran his fingers through his hair and straightened his vambraces. Checked that his belt was positioned just so.

'You have a bit of lipstick…' She demonstrated the spot by pointing to the area on her own face, but he got the wrong cheek. 'Other side.'

'Thanks. You have…'

He made a flapping motion with his hand that seemed to encompass her entire body.

'I'm in need of a mirror, yes. I'll see to it.'

'You look…'

'I *know.*'

'I was going to say beautiful. Better than any dream I've ever had.'

Oh.

'The phones never work up in the mountains where I'm going,' he said steadily as opened the door a crack. 'Look to the skies for my homing pigeons bearing news.'

CHAPTER SIX

IT WAS ALL very well to promise news and load up with homing pigeons to release at various stages on the journey—should other birds on the mountain be willing to leave them alone, but it was another issue altogether to try and write cramped little messages that were in any way meaningful.

Tomas was a man of very few words. He'd had more as a boy, but his trust in others had waned with Claudia's disappearance and been shattered when her father, the King, had refused to barter for her return. This new world with Casimir in charge was kinder, and the politics progressive, but Tomas still struggled to trust others—even his apprentices, who had proven themselves capable many times over. Giving him a barony and even *more* people to oversee just meant more work for him until he learned how to delegate.

Maybe he should write about that.

Today I thought about how to find staff for a manor house. And whether I seriously need to know what tableware to use for any given situation. Is this why I need two wives?

He couldn't finish a message there. Could he?

Mt. Saer: three golden eagle pairs, all plus eggs. On to Mt. Raeschi.

That would do. No need to overthink it, or to mention just how often he thought of Claudia's softness, her fierce strength, or the warm cradle of her body. Of course, there was always the slim chance the pigeon might not find its way home, but if it did his team had instructions to make sure the Princess Royal received the message.

A week later, something appeared in the sky that looked like no bird he'd ever seen. Something that startled his horses and made his falcons flap their wings in alarm. A drone. A drone, flying royal ribbons—it hovered in front of his face. This was a travesty. Gross misuse of airspace. Falcon fakery of the highest order. Maybe he'd club it to bits.

'Good morning, Master Falconer. Nice bushy beard you've got growing there.' Claudia's words rang out loud and clear.

'Why is this mechanical thing tracking me?'

'Well, I could hardly send a homing pigeon to you, now, could I? That's a one-way trip. Whereas this communication method…once the satellite picked up your coordinates, all I had to do was feed them into the program and hope for a sunny day. Marvellous, isn't it? Solar-powered. It's a military prototype.'

'I loathe it.'

'Hence the scowl, yes, I see. I was rather hoping you'd be impressed by my ingenuity.'

'The fact that he couldn't *see her* irritated him mightily.

'So, to answer your questions about the troubles inherent in having too many wives—I predict many, *many* troubles, too many to count. I don't recommend it.'

'You're not sitting in a room full of generals, are you? Because now would be a good time to tell me that.' He put his finger up against what he thought was the camera lens.

'Stop messing with my tech,' she ordered. 'Don't make me zap you. And there's no one else in the room with me. I'm the only one who can see and hear you.'

'That you know of,' he muttered darkly and kept his finger right where it was. There was nothing wrong with a little paranoia.

'You're going to need Lillis & Co pattern number PT12CBQ, white ribbed bone china, times twelve, plus banquet dishware. RWBee stainless steel cutlery plus full banquet mix additions for a table of eighteen. Veni glassware—crystalline with silver, design number CS32, and no one wants to skimp on glassware so you'll need the full set, meaning twenty-four of everything they can think of.'

'When you say "going to need…" Am I? Am I really? What if I've decided to be a no-frills baron with simple tastes?'

'I've sent you a list to look at when you return. You do intend to return to civilisation at some point?'

'Yes.' The drone rose into the air, dislodging his finger as it began to slowly circle him. 'That's cheating.'

'So, this is your camp.'

The drone stopped to hover over his tent and small campfire where three falcons perched unhooded—two of them with their bellies full of rabbit entrails, the third hungry and ready for flight. A pair of pigeons sat caged, awaiting release, and his three horses had been pegged out on a sweet grazing patch.

But had he sensed disapproval in her words rather than curiosity?

'What's wrong with it?'

'Needs more people. No one has your back.'

'I can protect myself.' He had enough hardware hidden on his person to stop single predators cold and a pump shotgun in the tent to defend against pack wolves. His birds and horses were more than capable of letting him know if he should be concerned by anything nearby. 'I'm not without survival skills.'

'That's so sexy.'

'I *really* hope no one's listening to you right now.'

'That I find you sexy isn't news. Find me someone of our acquaintance who *doesn't* know I'm hunting you and I'll show you a unicorn. Do you believe in unicorns, Tomas?' She sounded slightly wistful.

'I stay up here long enough, I start believing all sorts of things are possible,' he admitted gruffly. 'Although being tracked by a stolen military drone wasn't one of them.'

'Have you been thinking about us?'

'A lot.'

'I like honesty in a man. Also decisiveness. Are you ready to have dinner with me yet?'

'I thought we'd already established this as a possibility.'

'Hmm.' In no world would he ever mistake that little hum of hers as full agreement. 'Care to make it a certainty? When will you be back?'

'End of the month, maybe.' But he wasn't making promises. 'Depends what kind of reception I get in Aergoveny, and whether I think it's a good idea to interview for household staff and apprentices.'

'I like the way you're thinking.'

All this time on the mountain had at least clarified his dislike of having decisions made about his future from on high.

'I don't like being led, coaxed, cajoled, steamrolled, overruled—it's just the way I'm built. Your willingness to think you know what's good for me is a problem. It's not what I want in a lover, a partner or even a casual companion.' He wished he could see her face. Anything was better than the noise of the drone and Claudia's complete silence. 'I respect you and admire you. You're a powerful, influential individual who lobbies hard and gets results. But the very strengths that make you so effective in your brother's court are the same qualities that give me pause when I think about forming an *us*. We both like to be in charge.'

'I can...see how that might be a problem,' she said finally. 'I think, though—within the parameters of a sexual or romantic relationship, or both—that I wouldn't always need or want to be the one in control. It would be a relief not to be.'

Her answer floored him more thoroughly than the sudden appearance of a flying elephant would have.

'You might find the real me not to your liking,' she continued. 'But don't assume you know how I'll be if we enter a relationship. The Princess Royal you're basing your assessment on is a carefully crafted political weapon. There's more to me. And less. And I'm sorry I misunderstood your pigeon message. I took it as an invitation to engage. I didn't realise your next step would be to say sorry, not interested, but I'm not without ears. Message received.'

The drone rose.

'Wait!'

The drone hovered.

'I may have spent too much time with my own thoughts of late,' he admitted carefully. 'I still don't quite grasp what you want from me.'

'Same thing I've always wanted. A chance to know you properly, without artifice, titles or any other expectations getting in the way.' The little machine whirred and hummed. 'You said you needed a chance to think about it. If you've thought about it and don't want to take that chance, say so and I'll leave you to get on with your life. I *can* be told things I don't want to hear. I won't make your life difficult upon your return, if that's what you're worried about.'

He hadn't been worried about that at all.

'I don't even have to be there.'

'Claudia, stop. Can we start this conversation again?

This time without your push and my defensive indecision. I'll start.' He felt such a fool, talking to a machine, but he'd dug his own hole when it came to communicating with this forthright, challenging woman and it was up to him to find a way out of it. 'Would you like to have dinner with me when I get to Aergoveny? Either somewhere in the village if there's a tavern or restaurant or at my manor house if it's privacy you prefer.'

'There's a tavern,' she said. 'We could meet there and keep plans fluid. The only thing I will ask from you now is a date and time. My calendar fills up fast.'

'August the fourth at six p.m.'

'A full moon,' she said after a moment. 'A blue moon, in fact.'

He knew it. But then, it was his business to know the wax and wane of those things that affected the creatures in his care. 'Is that a problem?'

'Of course not. Makes for an interesting night. Your apprentices are getting used to me dropping in on them.'

'How's the little peregrine with the twisted toes?'

'She's with me now. The others were picking on her.'

'You imprinted her?'

'I took her with me when I visited a school group the other day and have yet to return her into general care. She's so sweet. There was a young girl there with twisted feet. Serendipity, but it started a discussion on limitations and potential and set me to thinking. What are your thoughts on putting together a travelling show for schools featuring little peregrine hatchling Suly and various other injured birds that the apprentices tell me can't be released and are permanently in your care?'

'I'll consider it, but only if you stop stealing my birds.' He probably shouldn't be smiling so hard. 'I start my new apprentices on those birds.'

'You take one new apprentice a year, Tomas.'

'And the years add up!' He currently had four. 'And I'm considering adding more.'

'I do hope you include girls in those interviews.'

'If they come, I consider them.'

'If you invite them, they will come.'

'Why does my brain hurt every time we talk?'

'It's expanding with possibilities.'

'No, I think it's you messing with me.' He knew it was.

The drone flew higher. 'You're smiling again.'

'I wish I could see your smile.' The words flew out before he could call them back. 'You sound insufferably smug.'

'I'll see you next blue moon. Don't be late because I will be there.'

'Can I shoot the drone now?' Because he was really, really itching to.

'You realise you could use one of these to get around all your golden eagle mating sites in an afternoon? You should get one.'

He withdrew his Ruger and took aim. Why on this glorious earth would he want to do that? 'I hate progress.'

It only took one shot.

Claudia had a stomach bug. A three-day wouldn't-go-away stomach bug that saw her lose the previous night's meal before breakfast each morning and made her feel like a marionette going through the motions the rest of the day. She'd tried keeping her distance from others lest they catch the bug too, but this morning Ana and Sophia had brought a breakfast tray to her room and sat with her while she sipped at the thin chicken broth in a porcelain cup and pushed dry toast soldiers around a pretty fluted plate.

'Why are you here? You'll catch it too,' Claudia protested for at least the tenth time.

Ana's smile was just that little bit too knowing, and Claudia knew just what she was thinking. 'I'm *not* what you think I am. I took a test.'

'A blood test?'

Well, no. She'd peed on a stick and heaved a giant sigh of relief when the result had come up negative. As it should have, because she'd had an injection against becoming pregnant some three…possibly four…months ago. She'd been well and truly *covered* when she and Tomas had temporarily lost their minds and joined bodies in the map room.

'It's impossible.'

'Been there, done that.' Ana smiled gently and reached for her cup of tea. 'Meet my daughter.'

'Hi,' said Sophia with a grin.

'I can't be that right now.' She couldn't even say the word—just thinking it was enough to make panic bloom. Tomas was still getting used to the idea of doing couple things in public, let alone aligning future goals. A future together—that she took great pleasure embellishing, in the privacy of her own mind—was in no way a sure thing. They hadn't even had their first date yet!

The thought of pressuring him into a relationship because she was pregnant only made her more nauseous.

She set the teacup down with a clatter and pushed the tray to the bottom of her bed, where Sophia sat watching with the innocent curiosity of childhood. Put a photo of Claudia at seven and Sophia at seven side by side and they could be mistaken for the same child. It was how Cas had known instantly that Sophia was his. He'd stopped at nothing—even kidnap—to bring Sophia under his roof so he could protect her and her mother, Ana. He'd been driven by fear and the need to protect them, and guilt too, for leaving Ana with no way to contact him. Claudia couldn't imagine her brother's emotions when he'd first set eyes on his daughter. He'd once said, over too many drinks, that he'd never felt more blessed and afraid in equal measure.

Watching her brother hold so tightly to Ana and Sophia in that revelatory press conference had sealed the deal when it came to Claudia returning to Byzenmaach after their father's demise. Not only would her return cement Casimir's claim on Sophia, he needed someone to help him make the most of the olive branch he'd publicly held out to the people of the north.

Claudia had real power now and changes were coming, and she could be proud of her role in bringing peace to her country. But with that role came certain expectations. Being unmarried, pregnant and unwilling to name the father would give her political opposition way too many clubs to beat her with.

'I can't be,' she repeated thinly. 'I have bigger responsibilities.' She deliberately avoided her niece's golden
gaze in case longing for a child of her own flooded
through her. 'Cas would—'

'Understand,' said Ana firmly.

Would he? He'd warned her to take it slow where
Tomas was concerned, but had she listened to his most
excellent advice? No.

She couldn't even begin to wrap her mind around
what Tomas might think. Or say. Or do, at this lack of
anything even resembling a controlled courtship and
emotionally steady way forward.

No.

Just no.

Ana removed the breakfast tray from the bed and set
it on the table by the window. She pulled the curtains
aside, her actions befitting a maid rather than the Queen
Consort. 'I'm here to support you.'

It was a strong position to take for someone who—a
year ago—had been a single working mother living an
ordinary life. Or maybe that experience was *why* Ana
was here. She knew Claudia would need allies if she
was...

Should she be...

Carrying.

'And what of Byzenmaach's broader population?
Would they support an unmarried pregnant princess? I
think not.' Claudia knew she sounded snappy. Maybe it
came of being half scared out of her mind.

'You're their Iron Princess. You're indestructible,'
Ana countered, turning back towards the bed. 'They'll
get used to it.'

'And then there's T—the father.' Last but emphatically not least. They'd never discussed children. They'd barely discussed dinner.

'Yes.' Ana's sympathetic gaze was almost too much to bear.

'He's not one to be trapped.' Understatement. 'He'll think I did it deliberately.'

'Maybe. Or he might trust that you wouldn't deliberately do such a thing.'

In her experience, trust was something that had to be earned.

'I let him think I was dead.'

'Due to circumstances beyond your control.'

Claudia liked this compassionate, clever woman who kept Cas grounded and worked so hard to be the figurehead her brother and this country needed. Even if her confidence in Claudia's ability to cultivate trust was misplaced.

'I pushed him out of his comfort zone.'

'He *is* rather rigidly self-contained. Probably do him good.'

'You don't even know who I'm talking about.'

Ana smirked and arched an elegant brow. Okay, she absolutely did.

'Of course, if you're not expecting, it won't matter what I know,' Ana said. 'Might be just a stomach bug. Shall I send the doctor up once she's finished with us?'

It wasn't the worst idea ever put forward, now, was it?

'Yes,' Claudia managed belatedly. 'Please. Let's put that fantasy to rest.'

CHAPTER SEVEN

Tomas rode into Aergoveny trailing two horses, three hawks and an empty pigeon cage. His arrival in the small mountain village did not go unnoticed. He'd been expecting a glance or two—the falcons always created interest and any newcomer to a place as isolated as this one was always greeted with some measure of suspicion. The silence as he dismounted in front of the only tavern didn't worry him as much as the smell of himself after spending so much time living rough. Hasty washes in almost frozen streams had barely taken the edge off the odour and he knew it. He had two days to get clean-shaven before Claudia arrived and he didn't know whether to take a room at the tavern or take his chances and keep going until he reached the property he now owned. Instinct suggested that, either way, it would be good manners to introduce himself, seeing as these villagers were soon going to be his neighbours.

The groom that rushed out to take his horses—shedding a serving apron along the way—was small, wiry and female. 'You're him,' she declared without preamble. 'The King's Falconer. We've been wondering when you'd turn up. The Princess Royal's people called two days ago and reserved a room for you, and the bathhouse and a barber. They said you'd scowl like that too. Da's inside and I can see to your horses. We've stables out back, with lowland hay and grain.' She looked longingly towards the falcons. 'I can take care of your birds too.'

'They don't leave my care.' Preferably his sight. 'They room with me.'

'Probably for the best. I saved a falcon once. The cats had it trapped and were going in for the kill and the stable doors were closed and it couldn't get out. It was exhausted, poor thing. I could pick it up and everything.'

Being showered with falcon stories was part and parcel of being the King's Falconer. It was his duty to listen and offer words of encouragement and advice. 'What happened to it?'

'I brought it inside and checked for wounds. It didn't have any I could see, but it wouldn't eat. Da said it was probably full of mice.'

Tomas and his animal entourage followed her to the stables, relieved when they were clean and warm, with wide stalls and several ponies already in residence. The girl slanted him a glance, took one of his packhorses, clipped it to a lead rope attached to a post and began to relieve the horse of its load. 'Use these three stalls here. They're ready for you.'

She knew her way around horses, and he joined her in the offloading.

'What happened to the bird?'

'We kept her overnight so she could recover her strength and then let her go.'

'Did you ever think about keeping her?'

'Dreamed of, more like,' the girl said with a snort.

'Why didn't you?'

'She was wild and grown and used to being free. Wouldn't have been fair. I'm Caitlin, by the way. Daughter of Bain, and hopefully wife of Balo one day—but don't tell him. He doesn't know yet.'

Tomas snorted. So did his horse. Poor Balo. 'Tomas.'

Such enthusiasm in her nod. 'I knew it! Who else would you be? The woman on the phone described you perfectly.'

'Did she now?' Surely Claudia wouldn't have been the one to make the call? She had aides for that. Didn't she?

'Big. Scowling. Shaggy dark hair and eyes you wouldn't dare disobey. And when he asks you to do something, you're moving before your brain even catches up.'

'Did she give you *her* name?'

'No.'

Could have been Lor having a laugh at his expense. 'You did the right thing with the wild falcon. You might have been able to train it to get used to you but you'd have never been able to trust it to return if you flew it.'

'I know.' She sounded wistful. 'That's what Da said.'

'I'll be interviewing for apprentices tomorrow.' Just like that, his mind was made up. 'I'll need at least half a dozen, maybe more.'

'Oh, man! The guys are going to go ape. Balo, okay? Remember the name!'

'Why not you?'

Her eyes widened with shock and excitement before she slowly, ruthlessly snuffed that light out. 'I work for

Da. He needs me more than you do.' She set his pack-saddle on a nearby table and returned her attention to the horse. 'Don't worry. You'll get plenty of interest. Is there an age range?'

'Not children—although I'll take falconry classes for children once the manor is up and running.' Go him. Being his own man and winging it and feeling good about it. And all because Claudia had challenged him to let go a little and loosen up on his emotions. He was doing it. 'Apart from that, anyone of any age can apply.'

'Do you need household workers too?'

'I'm thinking about it.' He'd make better decisions about that after he saw the place. He had ideas about open days to bring in income for running costs. Even the prize money he'd been given would run out eventually if he didn't figure out how not to bleed money when it came to running all the programmes he'd dreamed into existence while up in the mountains.

'I'll get the word out,' she offered.

'I'll do it myself.'

She wrinkled her nose and probably bit her tongue in an effort to keep her many opinions to herself.

'What now?' he grumbled.

'I mean, first impressions and all. You need a bath.'

The next day Tomas took interviews, got to know the people of Aergoveny. He'd sent word of his arrival to Claudia by text once his phone had recharged, and received a thumbs-up in reply.

He'd sent another short message about interviewing for apprentices and got a laughing smiley face in reply and nothing else. For a woman who had a lot to say in person and via drone, she was surprisingly circumspect by phone.

At six thirty-five on the morning of Claudia's arrival, he got a text from her.

Tomas, I have to cancel. I have a dreadful stomach bug and travel just isn't going to happen. You've got this!

He told her to get well soon in reply.

Maybe she really was sick with a rapid onset stomach complaint. Bad seafood at the royal banquet luncheon. A bad chicken wing during her afternoon snack.

He had to give her the benefit of the doubt.

He bundled up his disappointment into a tight ball and swallowed it whole, along with the breakfast on his plate. Claudia, the Princess Royal, had responsibilities to more than just him. She didn't owe him a longer explanation or for him to hear her voice while she explained away her absence. They were still at the start of a very long journey that could lead anywhere.

She didn't owe him anything.

The Aergoveny manor did nothing to curb Tomas's burgeoning dream of setting up a specialty raptor sanctuary. Situated in the middle of a hidden valley, surrounded by mountains, it stood harsh and plain, a grey fortress surrounded by high stone walls. A barren nest long since abandoned, but there was so much promise here, and the stonemasons and carpenters had made a good start on repairs. The stables were to the east, along with entrance gates and bunkhouses. The aviaries were to the west. The kitchen garden and orchard lay to the south and consisted mainly of weedy garden beds and ragged fruit trees that had once been espaliered against protective stone walls. What a place to train birds to the glove!

He could see it already. This tiny jewel in the Byzenmaach crown could one day become a raptor breeding and rehabilitation centre that could easily earn its way by putting on open days and re-enactment fairs and providing education opportunities for children in the summer months. If he wanted company in the main house, it could potentially accommodate a handful of environmental researchers and ornithologists all year round.

He claimed a room on the ground floor near the kitchens for his meagre belongings, and maybe one day he'd graduate to feeling comfortable inhabiting the master bedroom but that day had yet to come. He spent another week organising aviary repairs and ordering materials and trying not to read anything into the fact that Claudia hadn't contacted him.

He invited Silas and Lor and stablemaster Ivan from the winter fortress to visit and give their opinions on staffing and maintenance, ever grateful for their cheerful support and practical experience. He moved back and forth between the fortress and his new home for another two weeks, running himself ragged trying to do his job and oversee the work happening in Aergoveny.

For a man who'd objected so strongly to becoming a baron, he wasn't lost to the fact that he was wholeheartedly *embracing* the reality of it.

Claudia was right. Having the freedom to build something for *himself* was addictive.

He wasn't actively trying to avoiding Claudia but she was never in residence when he returned home, and on the one occasion he'd asked Lor where she was, Lor had got the strangest look on her face and muttered something about her being tied up at the palace while multinational water negotiations took place.

It sounded perfectly reasonable. There was no earthly reason for him to suspect something was off.

Claudia was an important woman.

Lor had never steered him wrong.

And yet, if a falcon in his care had prompted this kind of uneasy feeling he'd be keeping it under close observation.

When the royal helicopter landed at the fortress that afternoon, he thought he might get his chance to catch up with Claudia that evening, but the helicopter spat out Ana and young Sophia and no one else.

To say he hid his resulting foul mood from his apprentices would be a lie. He tried to limit the damage done by giving them all an impromptu half day respite from general chores. Instead, he asked them to go home and write a two-page response to the idea of rotating them in and out of the Aergoveny manor one or two at a time for one or two months at a time while he continued to travel between the two sites. He needed people he could trust at both places, needed them to provide continuity of care for the birds and alert him to any problems. Two of his apprentices had young families to consider, two didn't. No one would be penalised for speaking out against such a move. No one would lose their apprentice-ship. They should consider their two-page spiels to be expressions of interest, or disinterest. He simply wanted to know what their circumstances would allow.

The silence that followed his announcement wasn't encouraging.

Finally, his fourth-year apprentice spoke up. 'What are *your* long-term intentions? As the King's Falconer and now lord of your own lands?'

'I intend to expand the King's falcon breeding pro-grammes and open up the Aergoveny manor to the pub-lic. I'm looking into housing other endangered birds and eventually reintroducing them into areas where re-searchers think they will survive. There will be monitor-ing programmes. Research opportunities. Learning and exchange of ideas because I sure as the sky don't know everything. I know you're all encouraged to leave at the end of your four years here. I know you can count on finding key positions worldwide. And if your goals and dreams have always lain elsewhere, I say go for them. I'm setting you up for success *anywhere*.' He meant every word. 'But I'm opening up two permanent po-sitions immediately as part of my goals for the future. One here, one in Aergoveny. Maybe even four perma-nent Master Falconer positions in the years to come, and four apprenticeships offered each year. I've been given a sackful of money and the most beautiful raptor sanc-tuary location in the world and I'm going for it.'

Silence greeted his words. Silence, sideways glances and finally grins.

'Whatever you want done, I'll do it,' his fourth-year apprentice replied firmly. 'I want in on the ground floor.'

'Mad not to,' said his third-year apprentice. 'Count me in too.'

'And me,' said Bran, the youngest, hurriedly. 'I have family in Aergoveny. My father grew up there. I'll go there any time and be happy about it.'

'And I'll go with him.' His remaining apprentice smiled broadly. 'Have you *seen* his cousin? She's the prettiest woman in the world and sweet along with it.'

'She lives in the capital, Romeo,' countered Bran.

'And when she returns to visit her family, I will be standing there flying falcons and looking majestic by association. King's Falconer's apprentice. Never fails to impress.'

Bran puffed up like a little barnyard rooster. 'That's an unfair advantage!'

Bran had been using that unfair advantage to devastating effect ever since he'd got here. Tomas didn't bother to disguise his smirk.

'Are you sure you're all with me?' He hadn't expected such instant support. Was leadership always this easy with a vision in mind and the resources to make it happen? 'Thank you, I'm humbled.' He was also hungry to see what could be achieved and how fast they could begin to make it happen when working as a team and taking on extra responsibilities. 'I'll have new employment contracts for you to look over by the end of the week. I still want your thoughts on rotation planning. Add a paragraph on what you're most looking forward to being part of. I'll take looking *majestic by association* as a given.'

He was still smiling at that one later that afternoon when his apprentices were long gone and he was finishing the last of the weigh-ins and deciding that the time had come to properly embrace computer records in addition to the trusty notebooks that had served his father and grandfather so well. Especially now that birds and people would be travelling back and forth between sites.

He saw Sophia pause in the doorway to the weighing room, her trusty wolfhounds Jelly and Belly at her side. He saw her raise her tiny fist to knock on the doorframe and then pause, her gaze shifting from him to the eyas on the tray in front of him. Best not to knock right now and startle them. He liked the way she'd paused to think about that. Another falconer in the making, he decided with no little satisfaction.

'You can come closer if you're quiet,' he murmured. 'Make the hounds sit by the door.'

The King's daughter did exactly that as he recorded the weight. 'Do you want to feed her?' he asked of the bird in his hand.

'Yes, please.'

He pointed towards the bucket of meat and nodded. He liked this little girl with her affinity for animals and Claudia's eyes, even if it had taken some getting used to her. It had been like seeing a ghost at first, and he hadn't been the only one to think so. Cas had been blindsided by his daughter's resemblance to Claudia too.

Claudia's presence had gone a long way to making Tomas regard young Sophia as a person in her own right. It wasn't Sophia's fault that her looks and mannerisms sometimes left him spinning with memories of his childhood and Claudia's.

He would do better by this child. They all would.

For starters, young Sophia knew her parents loved her and cared for her as they should.

'Does she weigh enough?' the little girl asked.

'Yes. See how the numbers on the chart keep going up slowly but surely? That's what we want to see.'

'How old is she?'

'Four weeks.'

He answered more questions while she helped him weigh the next set of hatchlings. He watched her eyes grow round when he told her he was thinking about placing one with a young woman in Aergoveny whose main job was to help her father run a tavern. He thought the young woman had a way with animals and people too, and he wanted to teach her and many others the art of falconry and experience the practical partnerships between people and birds.

'I want to experience the practical partnerships too,' Sophia assured him earnestly.

'It takes a lot of time. And right now you're learning other big skills. Don't you have a new pony to ride and a wolfhound puppy coming soon?'

Sophia nodded.

'Show me how well you care for them, over and over for years, and we can talk again about getting you your own hatchling.'

'Aunt Claudia had a falcon of her own when she was seven.'

'Did she now?'

'And so did you. Aunt Claudia told me.'

'*Did* she now?'

'She says you were her best teacher ever.'

Ha. 'I was eleven at the time and my father was teaching us both. It's good to learn things alongside a friend.' He hoped his new apprentices proved his words true.

'So you and Aunt Claudia are friends. Is that why she doesn't want to trap you?'

'What do you mean?'

'With a baby.'

She wasn't making sense. 'A—*what*?'

'Aunt Claudia's baby. In her belly.'

Still not computing. He lifted the last of the eyas off the scales and back into the bucket, and wrote the weight down in the record book. Miracle of miracles, his hands stayed steady throughout.

'Aunt Claudia has a baby in her belly?'

The little girl nodded.

'Did she say that?' He should be ashamed, pumping a child for information, but here they were.

Another nod. 'And then my father said, "He needs to know" and Aunt Claudia said, "Why would I trap him when he's just been set free?" and my father said, "It's your duty to tell him" and that's when they really started yelling.'

'So you overheard this conversation but you weren't part of it.' Sophia was beginning to look scared. He hadn't raised his voice but if he could track the tight tension in his words, doubtless so could she.

'Am I in trouble?'

'Not with me.' He tried to make his voice sound less harsh as he crouched in front of her. 'No, but princesses have rules they need to live by. And one of the first rules of princessing is that you don't repeat conversations you're not part of in the first place. You might be giving secrets away to the wrong people.'

'Indeed,' said a voice from the doorway, and there stood Ana, her pretty face grave as she stared down at them. He straightened, crossed his arms for good measure and held his Queen's gaze with a flinty one of his own.

'Thank you, Tomas. I can take it from here. Come on, Soph.' Ana held out her hand for her daughter to take. 'Let's get you cleaned up for dinner. Your father will be joining us.'

He hadn't started this conversation but, one way or another, he would hear the end of it. 'Will the Princess Royal be joining you too?'

'Do you have business with her?'

'You tell me.'

Ana was the first to look away. 'With the water rights negotiations completed, she was heading north with Lord Ildris for a time. To celebrate.'

'Ildris's horses are here.'

'I believe they flew. Lord Ildris will be returning at the beginning of next week. He's accepted a permanent consultancy position within the palace.'

More fool Cas.

'Did you just…*growl*?' asked Sophia with no little fascination.

'I'm sure the Lord Falcon Master was just clearing

his throat,' Ana murmured. 'As for the Princess Royal, I believe she's staying up north for a week or two longer, maybe more. The mountains were calling.'

He had mountains. He had mountains on his *door-step*. This very fortress had been carved into the side of one, should anyone want to get pedantic about their proximity to shouty big blocks of stone.

'Come on, Soph. Time to go.' Ana ushered her daughter to the door but spared him a glance at the very last moment. 'You speak mountain man, don't you?'

CHAPTER EIGHT

IT WAS COLD in the north. Claudia had forgotten the icy bite of the wind on any part of her not covered by wind and waterproof clothing. Not for this place the ball-gowns and jewels of her brother's palace. Not for these people the unbearable judgement because she was too confident, too immune to bribery and way too satisfied with her own good self to be of use to those who thought blackmail a legitimate political tool, just as long as it served their greater good.

Or maybe these people of the north had been there and done that with her already and figured she could use a break.

She was second-guessing everything about her world and the people in it. Why not second-guess them too?

Only the doctor, Ana, Cas, Sophia and probably Lor knew she was pregnant, but it wouldn't be long before solid rumours started swirling. A small but powerful group of politicians and courtiers from her father's era had already called for her removal from Cas's court. They said she'd been seduced by the northerners and pressured into being their voice, as if she'd never had a conscience of her own. They called her a survivor of abuse, as if the abuse had originated with her captors rather than her parents. They underestimated her strength and her influence, those little men and women with their fat bank accounts and political portfolios and no interest whatsoever in fairness. They would pull her down at the earliest opportunity if she couldn't find the strength to withstand them.

Unfortunately, she spent most of her strength these days on getting up in the morning and staying up rather than crawling straight back into bed after a bathroom stop, her mind a fog and her body not her own to command. What did she know about motherhood and babies? Her own mother had been a shadow of a woman—pitiful and broken. Her so-called father—King Leonidas—had been a monster. Her real father had thought nothing of bedding his brother's wife. What kind of a family tree was that?

As for the people who'd kidnapped and then kept a small child out of pity and a vague idea that one day they could use her to advance themselves, she'd paid them back, hadn't she? She'd secured their rights and way of life and owed them nothing more. She was square with them now. Surely they could ask for nothing more?

And maybe they wouldn't want her around now she'd served her purpose, but she had nowhere else to turn to for comfort and support and possible solutions to a problem of her own making.

Why did she no longer know which way was home?

She'd been welcomed with fanfare. Her tent had been set up for her, bursting with warmth and furs and food after her journey. She'd been hugged and lauded—she and Ildris heroes. A feast was happening right outside her door.

And all she could think was that she didn't belong here either. She wouldn't wish this duality on her enemy, let alone her daughter, and since when had this baby become a daughter? She didn't know that for sure. No one did.

'Claudia, are you in there?'

She knew that voice. It belonged to her not-sister who'd been at Claudia's side since they were seven years old. 'Enter.'

Alya entered with a flurry of movement and a dusting of snow on her hair and the shoulders of her cloak. 'Why are you missing the party? You're the guest of honour.'

'Just tired, I guess.'

'You guess or you know? Because unless you haven't slept in days, I'm going to drag you back out there. People want to see you. You're our champion.'

'I'm pregnant.' There. She'd said it, but didn't feel any lighter for sharing her load. If anything, she was waiting for the weight of Alya's disappointment to rain down upon her.

Alya pushed back her hood, bringing her ebony curls, heart-shaped face and shocked brown eyes into the light. 'Oh.'

Yes, oh.

'Change of plan on the drinking front,' Alya said next.

'Indeed.'

'And I guess it explains why you're looking so pale and worn.'

'More than likely.' And she'd tried so hard to add a bit of colour using make-up.

'Do I, ah, know the father?'

'You mean is Ildris the father? No, of course he's not.'

'Is that because he's too old for you?'

'Twelve years isn't that big an age gap if plenty of other things align. It's because I don't care for him in that way and never have, no matter how handy he is to have in my corner. No, Ildris knows nothing about it.' Or maybe he knew more than she thought. He was a secretive soul, more suited to politicking than she would ever be. 'I slept with the King's Falconer.'

'You mean…you slept with Tomas? The boy hero?'

She could blame childhood confidences on Alya knowing all about him.

'What can I say? He grew up well.'

Alya shed her cloak and took a seat at Claudia's table, reached for the untouched wine and poured herself a glass. She reached for a sweet pastry too, giving every indication that she wasn't going anywhere. 'Does he know?'

'No. It was a one-off. I was being my usual pushy self. I don't even know if he wanted to be naked with me in the first place.' Not that he *had* been naked.

'He can't have been too much against bedding you if he got the deed done.'

'I can be very persuasive.'

'Given that we're out there celebrating that very fact… I know.' Alya waved her hand with the pastry in it towards the tent flap, before popping the honey-soaked confection in her mouth.

'I don't think this is the result he would want if given a choice,' Claudia confessed baldly.

The other woman chewed thoughtfully and then reached for her wine, taking her time. 'Choice is a luxury some people don't get to have. You of all people know that.'

'I can choose not to implicate him.' She'd been thinking about that avenue a lot.

'No man worth a hero badge is going to let you get away with that if he thinks that baby's his. He's going to want to be there for that child. Maybe he'll want to be there for you too. Let's call that *his* choice.'

'You're saying I should tell him?'

The other woman nodded. 'If you're keeping it, yeah.'

'I'm keeping her.'

'Oh, it's a *her*, is it?'

'Only in my stupid head.' Claudia felt hot tears start to well. 'I don't even *like* my role at the palace. The public are fed this notion that I'm this indestructible princess, back from the dead. Some kind of icon, preferably in a tiara, only the more people get to know me, the more they realise I'm just human and I make mistakes. Fitting in is tough. Cas wants me there but has warned me to back off on some of my advocacy until I'm more settled. Even my parentage is in question—my real father was likely the man I thought was my uncle, which is why Leonidas never wanted my return. And now I'm pregnant. How is that helpful? My position is so precarious. I don't know how I'm going to be of use to *anyone* going forward.'

'Hush, Claudia. You can always stay here. We'll have you, and gladly.'

'Will you? Or have I delivered on the water rights and now you're done with me too?'

'See, that's just crazy mixed-up baby hormones talking,' Alya said firmly. 'Come back outside and I'll *show* you that's not true. People are in awe of what you have achieved. We love you and we've missed you.'

'I don't know what I'm doing or where I'm going.' She was a compass dial, endlessly circling. 'I don't know which way's home.'

Alya rose and embraced her. 'I'll help you find the way. I'll come with you on that journey, but be warned, I'm going to be the naughty auntie.'

Claudia clutched her honorary sister's hand and clung with all her might. 'Thank you.'

'Don't thank me yet. I'm going to be a very bad influence. The stories I can tell about what we got up to as kids. There's the stolen pony story.'

'Rescued pony.' Claudia smiled through her tears.

'The duck egg substitution story. That was one very confused owl.'

'I now have a great deal of sympathy for that owl. I'd be confused too if this baby turned out to be a duckling.'

Alya squeezed tight and then gently stepped away. 'Rug up and come back to the feast, at least for a little while. Let's celebrate new beginnings and the peace and prosperity on the horizon. I won't even mention your part in the negotiations if you don't want me to. You can watch me try and fail to catch Ildris's attention. It'll be like old times.'

'He's taken a position in Cas's court.'

'I know.' For all that Alya tossed those two words around lightly, there was heartbreak behind them. 'Don't remind me. I too am not all that happy with reality today. Shall we face it anyway?'

This was the attitude that had guided her way. *Try*, and know that failure was part of that process. Be *honest*, with yourself if no one else.

'I want Tomas to be with me because he wants to be, not just because there's a baby. I'm afraid he's going to offer marriage and I'm going to say yes, and I'm never going to know how he really feels about me.'

'I get it. You're screwed. He's screwed too. But, whatever happens, I say this baby is going to be incredibly lucky to have you for a mother, because you have so much love and passion to give, and you're strong and fierce and capable of making life *better* for everyone around you. Forged in fire and all that. Be proud of your remarkable journey through life in search of your happy place. One day you're going to find it. You've got this.'

'You make me feel better than I've felt in weeks.'

'That's because I know what you need.' Alya stood and linked her arm around Claudia's. 'Come outside for a while and let us love you.'

'One hour, and then I'm coming back in.'

'One hour,' the other woman agreed. 'And I'll bring you breakfast in the morning.'

'I don't do breakfast any more.'

Alya's glance was full of concern. 'When do you breakfast, and what will tempt you to eat?'

'Around eleven and soup is good. Thin and brothy.'

'Have you seen a midwife? Let's do that tomorrow.'

'Tomorrow,' agreed Claudia, relaxing just a little bit. Maybe things would be better tomorrow.

Claudia lasted an hour, and then another, with Alya at her side, bubbling over with festive good humour and cloaking Claudia's forced enthusiasm. She *was* glad to be back, even if she knew in her heart that her status here had changed and there was no going back to her old life. Not easily. She had become a creature of politics, with the same pressure here as the one she felt in her brother's court, namely that she couldn't please everyone all the time. And what then? Who would even want her?

Bleakness had bled into her bones and she didn't know how to reverse the condition.

She'd settled before the open fire, Ildris to one side and Alya on her other as the celebrations continued and the fire began to show a hint of embers. There were a million stars above her head, a cloudless sky and a waxing crescent moon. She had shelter nearby and warmth on her face and there was simple comfort in that.

Take the simple, fleeting moments of comfort and security and be grateful, Claudia.

Make every breath, every moment, count. Just like old times.

She didn't know at first why Ildris rose to his feet so suddenly. It was late, she was weary, and she'd begun to let her mind drift.

But a woman was heading towards them and behind her strode Tomas, big and solid and contained as only he could be. He wore ordinary outdoor work boots and trousers and a warm winter jacket with wide cuffs made of leather. The firelight did little to soften the sharply drawn planes of his face and jaw, and his eyes were narrowed and not just against the smoke from the fire. He was set against Ildris, regular observation had told her that much, but he was usually somewhat better at hiding it. Hostility had a hold on him now, though. And then he saw her, and his hostility increased tenfold.

Maybe Ildris wasn't the problem after all.

'Well met, Master Falconer, Lord Sokolov,' Ildris began. 'What brings you amongst us?'

'I'm here for what's mine, mountain lord, and you can object to my claim, but know that I'm already disposed to think of you as my enemy. My grievance spans *decades*.'

Alya squeaked, Ildris crossed his arms in front of him and held his ground as Claudia scrambled to her feet and stepped between the two foes. 'Have you lost your mind?' she demanded.

'Not yet. Have you?' The next minute, she was viewing the world upside down on account of being slung over Tomas's shoulder, bottom up and head down, as he strode away from the fire, the crowd parting for him like butter, with him the hot knife.

'Are you kidnapping me?'

'Yes. You should be used to it by now. Or I could be rescuing you, or saving your life, who would know?'

'You! You should know what you're doing! And you can't just take me. You're outnumbered. People will stop you.'

'They can try.' Tomas gave a piercing whistle, the

one he used to call birds down from flight, and a short time later she heard the flapping of wings as a majestic golden eagle landed on his outstretched forearm.

She looked up. The bird looked down. 'Oh, aren't you a beauty,' she cooed. 'Tomas, where have you been hiding *her*?'

'Stop trying to win over my attack bird.' He had his hands full so there was nothing to stop her rooting around in the pocket of his trousers for a strip of dried meat that would surely be stuffed somewhere on his person.

Front pocket, deep, deep down.

Hello.

'Feed my bird that particular bit of meat and I may not be able to forgive you,' he warned.

A man of humour, how lovely. Claudia withdrew, but not before trailing admiring fingers along his delectable length. She found the food in his inside coat pocket and held it out for the eagle, praying that her odd position and all the jostling about as she held the food up for the bird wouldn't encourage it to take a finger as well.

'What's her name?'

'Never you mind.'

'Claudia!' Alya had come up beside them, almost running to keep apace as she bent to look Claudia in the eyes. 'What's happening?'

'I'm being kidnapped.' Claudia felt oddly cheerful. 'But thanks for asking.' Tomas still hadn't broken his stride. 'Alya, meet Tomas. Tomas, Alya.'

But the other woman was having nothing to do with

formal introductions and Tomas didn't seem that interested either.

'Do you *want* to be kidnapped?' Alya sounded anx-
ious.

'I'm thinking about it.' The eagle took the meat. Her
fingers stayed attached to her hand.

'Because if you need saving, I'll save you. His neth-
ers are currently unprotected. He'll likely drop you and
the eagle will pluck out my eyes, but I'll do it.'

'And I will never forget such a beautiful offer,' Claudia assured her just as earnestly. 'But I'm very comfortable, really.'

Tomas made a noise that sounded a lot like pure frustration, and Alya squeaked again. 'Did he just *growl*?'

'He does that. And yet I've still decided I'm willing
to be kidnapped. Again. Or rescued. Or taken to dinner. Whatever.'

'If you're sure…'

'I can paddle your backside if you don't take this more
seriously,' Tomas warned.

Ha! Stretch goal. 'What with? Your third arm?' They
were slowing down. They'd reached the edge of the
camp, where a group of horses were staked out. 'Are
you planning on stealing horses for us too? Because I'm
not sure you'll get away with *that*.'

'He shouldn't push his luck,' agreed Alya.

'I brought the Range Rover.' He deposited her on her
feet and opened the back doors and set about contain-
ing his golden eagle.

Claudia took a moment to embrace the sister of her
heart. 'I'll be fine,' she whispered.

'He's glorious,' Alya whispered back.

'I know. Good luck with Ildris. He was not tempted by anyone in the capital and you've more than enough soft power and courage to make him a very good match.'

'If you've quite finished planning the next generation of leaders,' said Tomas from behind them. 'Well met, Lady Alya. Princess, we're leaving now.' He opened the front passenger door and handed her in and buckled the seatbelt for her, and was it her imagination or did his hand linger over her stomach? Did he know? Was that the reason for all the theatrics? The very definitive swooping in to take what was his?

'Tomas…' She couldn't hide the hesitation in her voice.

'Not now.'

Call me, mimed Alya as the door closed. Claudia heard more voices outside and then he was getting in the driver's side and starting the engine. Her bravado—what was left of it—fizzled away, leaving only the occasional bubble of confidence in a sea of flat bewilderment.

Five minutes went by in silence. Ten. Another ten. Apparently, he'd used up all his words when claiming her. He didn't seem at all eager to reveal why he'd done so.

'Why did you come for me?'

He didn't glance her way. Never even took his eyes off the road ahead, but his hands tightened on the wheel and the tension in his body was contagious. 'Because you have something to tell me.'

He knew. Somehow, he'd discovered her condition.

'Who told you?'

'Sophia.'

Hard to take revenge on a little girl.

'And you think it's yours?'

He spared her a scathing glance. 'Don't even try that line. It won't hold.'

Possibly not. Everyone knew where her interest lay.

'My head was covered last time I was kidnapped. My hands were tied and travel was by horseback. This is a luxury abduction by comparison.'

'There are blankets and pillows on the back seat.'

Now he was making her feel ungrateful.

'I would have told you.' Maybe. 'Eventually.'

'Big of you.'

'I'm not trying to make the problem go away, if that's what you're worried about.'

'It's not a *problem*, it's a baby.' Oh, he could sound vicious when he wanted to.

'Right. I'm not trying to make this baby go away. I'm adjusting to its unexpected presence. I *was* protected. I thought I was. It wasn't a trap.' She wanted to make that clear. 'I'm…' Would honesty suffice? Could she say she was scared this baby would ruin her life and his? 'I'm trying to get my head around what it means, going forward. I took some time to shore up my defences.'

Nothing.

'Where are we going?' she asked, mainly to fill that awful silence with something other than tension.

'Home.'

She laughed, short and sharp. 'You might need to factor in the Claudia effect. Too bold for my brother's court.

A weapon spent as far as the north is concerned. I have no home. I seem to have run out of options.'

'I'm taking you to the manor. And if it's not home to either of us yet, I trust that in the years to come it will be. A bolthole like the room we had in the fortress wall. *Our* place. A safe place. We can make it happen this time.'

Oh, those words and the memories that followed. The promise of safety was her Achilles heel.

'We'll be married as soon as it can be arranged,' he added gruffly.

It wasn't a question, but still…

'You want to marry me?'

'Who knows?' He hadn't looked at her once. 'But there's a baby coming so we're doing it. It's the only way.'

Dogged chivalry. Not that there was anything wrong with it, but it wasn't love, and it was love she craved, almost as much as safety.

'Actually, there are many other ways to approach impending parenthood.' Probably best not to say *impending doom*. 'You've had a shock, I understand that, but what if I don't *want* to marry you?'

'I think you'll choose to do so anyway.' Was that the voice of reason? She hated it. 'Our child will be legitimate and loved and I will protect you both with all that I am. Any political opponents that seek to undermine you will suffer for their sins because I'm a vengeful man and my aristocratic veneer is thin.'

Well, when he put it that way…

'You're quite a forceful guy when you decide you want something.'

He smiled tightly. 'I have no idea why you sound so surprised.'

'I like it.'

'How fortunate for us all.'

She fiddled with the delicate ring on her finger, a diamond and pearl Art Deco concoction from the royal collection. She had a few vague memories of her mother wearing it, and it served to keep her tethered to her duties as the Princess Royal of a nation. The thought of wearing Tomas's wedding ring alongside it gave her pause, because she knew she would treasure his ring more.

'Do you even like me?' She hadn't meant to voice the question. She'd meant to keep those doubts locked in her subconscious, hidden from scrutiny. Clearly, her heart had other ideas. 'I mean, it's a starting point, right? Liking each other.'

'Correct.'

'I'd take my wedding vows seriously,' she said next. 'I'd give it my all.'

'As would I.'

'I'd take no other lovers.'

'Fewer bodies for me to bury.'

'I can't quite tell if you're being serious or not.'

He smiled at that, wide and wicked. What a weapon. It made her feel all jelly, not that he needed to *know* that.

'Still can't tell,' she informed him loftily.

'I'd probably just feed them to the birds. No grave-digging at all.'

'The fact that you've even thought about feeding people to the birds is giving me pause.'

'So it should.' He'd relaxed his grip on the steering wheel and his upper body looked less stiff. 'I'm joking. But I'm also a proud, possessive man and I don't share. If I'm going to surrender to my emotions, I aim to do it properly. I'm calling it the Claudia effect.'

And, oh, how she adored this accessible new side of him.

'So, it's a proper marriage you're suggesting. None of this in-name-only business.'

'Definitely not.'

'What happens when I have to do my brother's bidding and be a princess for the people?'

'Do you *want* to do your brother's bidding and be a princess for the people? Because, to my way of thinking, you give them too much unfettered access. With a child on the way, I'd expect you to pick your battles carefully and create more time for personal home-building.'

'At your manor.'

'*Our* manor. Correct.'

She was beginning to feel very hopeful about this unexpected kidnapping with marriage attached.

'I hear make-up sex is really intense. We should try it.'

'I'm sure we will.'

'Although not too often,' she hastened to add. 'Upon reflection, sex with you is already intense enough. I loved it.' Maybe if she used the word love around him enough his subconscious would get the hint and associate the word with her. She closed her eyes and conjured the memory of him striding towards her in the light of the campfire. His certainty. His utter willingness to stride into camp and claim her, as if he had every right to do so and an army at his back. 'The golden eagle was an exceptionally nice touch,' she murmured sleepily. She hadn't slept well for days, possibly weeks, and for the first time in weeks she wanted to surrender to the dark, knowing that Tomas would be there when she woke. 'What's her name?'

'Alhena.'

'You named her after a star.'

'I did.'

'You'll wake me when we get there? It's just… I'm so tired.'

'Then sleep.'

She loved his voice, his presence, everything about him. 'Don't make me wake alone.' She remembered that from her long-ago abduction, and the terror that had invaded her soul. 'I don't like waking up alone in a strange place.'

'I won't let you wake up alone.'

'Promise me.' She barely knew what she was saying. Fatigue had a hold on her now, slurring her words and robbing her of caution. 'I'm scared I've done you wrong and that you'll come to your senses and leave.'

'On my word, you won't wake up alone.'

Tomas drove through the night and kept his eyes on the road, never mind that they felt full of ash and grit. He'd never carried a more precious cargo. He'd never felt more sure that this was the road they should be on. No matter the fallout—and he expected plenty—he could not sit back and do nothing, not this time. He had another chance to do right by Claudia of Byzenmaach and he would not let her down. Not this time.

Claudia roused only briefly when he pulled over and took the pillows and blanket from the back and tried to make her sleeping position more comfortable. Was this normal? Was he going to spend the next many months worrying about her health and that of the baby she carried, and doing everything in his power to make her feel at home?

Yes…yes, he was.

He called Caitlin and arranged a room at the tavern, and a hearty breakfast for two, and said he'd be there in the early hours of the morning, and that he wouldn't usually ask for someone to be waiting up for him but it couldn't be helped. He'd pay double the rate. Triple.

'Da sleeps light, Lord Falconer. Will you have birds and horses with you again?'

'Just a golden eagle.'

'Holy sh—moley!'

'Are you sure you don't want to be one of my apprentices?'

'If wishes were horses, Da would be able to afford to employ enough people to replace me. Then I could.'

'If the opening of the manor brings in enough people, Aergoveny will grow and he'll be able to.'

'Keep dreaming, my lord, and so will I. Come in the side door closest to the stables. There's parking there. Gotta go. Tables won't clear themselves and it's Friday night.'

She rang off before he could murmur his thanks. Claudia stirred as he reached out to turn the phone off—

he didn't like those things tracking him, and no one could tell him they weren't. He caught the gleam of her eyes in the dashboard lights.

'Who was that?' she murmured.

'I called the tavern in Aergoveny. They're keeping a room for us.'

'But who were you speaking to? It sounded like you knew them.'

'The innkeeper has a daughter, Caitlin. She's about, I don't know, fifteen or so. Does the work of three people, alongside her father. She has the best instinct for my birds that I've ever seen since, well, since you.'

'Did you offer her an apprenticeship?'

He nodded. 'She considered it for a wistful heartbeat and then informed me she couldn't be spared. She probably can't. But circumstances can change.' He tried to gauge how Claudia was feeling after her two-hour nap, but the low light made it difficult. 'How are you feeling? There's water here and some of Lor's sweet pastries.'

'Maybe later. You said we were going to the manor. Why are we now staying at an inn?'

'Changed my mind when I remembered I only had tinned beans and bitter coffee in the cupboard. This way, you'll get breakfast.'

'It really wouldn't have mattered,' she offered dryly, sitting up straighter, tucking her hair away from her face and looking out of the window at the darkness thrown by a quarter moon and a cloudless night. 'How far away are we?'

'We'll be there in an hour.'

'I need to call Cas. Ildris vouched for my safety when

we went north and I don't know where my guards are. I don't want to start another war.'

'Call him by all means, but your guards are a couple of miles behind us and have been all the time. Cas knows where you are, even if he doesn't know the why of it yet.' Silently, he gestured towards his phone. 'You'll have to turn it on again and hope for a signal. And it'll come up as me when you dial anywhere so don't expect to have a direct line to the King.'

'Okay.'

Casimir picked up on the first ring.

'Huh,' she murmured. 'I guess you have a direct line to the King now too. Fancy that.' She put the phone on loudspeaker—a courtesy Tomas hadn't expected. 'Cas, I'm with Tomas.'

'So I heard. Ildris says your abduction was quite the spectacle.'

'I enjoyed it,' she answered dulcetly. 'We're almost in Aergoveny. My fiancé—that would be Tomas—has arranged a night at the inn for us before we travel on to the manor.'

'So you've told him about the baby.'

'Well, *someone* told him and I confirmed it, so yes. Let's not sweat the details. He knows. We're eloping. Think of the money you'll save.'

'I see.' Cas didn't sound impressed.

'As if you've never got ahead of yourself,' she reminded him.

'Put him on.'

'I can't, he's driving. Very safely, I might add, if I wanted to ram home the point that I'm in good, safe hands. We're working out our future and it's a delicate negotiation, as you might imagine. Can you tell the guards to keep their distance?'

'You wouldn't be sitting there if I hadn't already done so.'

'You're a wonderful brother. The best.'

'I'm glad you think so. I'm also Byzenmaach's King, so put your fiancé on the phone and turn the speaker off. I want a private word.'

She hesitated. Tomas didn't, reaching out to pick up a set of earphones from the console and handing them to her. She gave it all back, set up for privacy, and he sighed and put the earbuds in his ears. He'd known he was pushing his luck. It was a measure of the King's trust in him that no one had yet interfered. He wanted to keep it that way.

'Your Majesty.'

'Ballsy move, Lord Sokolov.'

'Unavoidable. Your sister was being uncommonly indecisive.'

'That or she's playing the long game and has you exactly where she wants you.'

'Maybe.' He hadn't ruled that out. 'Makes no difference to me. I need special dispensation to wed. The innkeeper's a celebrant.' He'd discovered that on his last visit. 'It can happen tonight if required.'

'Hey!' said Claudia indignantly. 'That is *not* required.'

Tomas liked to think he quelled her with a glance, but it seemed unlikely. 'Tomorrow, then.' Look at him, changing his plans at a moment's notice. And they called him intractable.

'Sunday,' she countered.

Two days away.

'Your sister says we're marrying on Sunday. I say to-morrow *evening*.' There he went, being tractable *again*. He shot Claudia a swift narrow-eyed glance. 'That's it. I'm done negotiating.'

'I'll clear my weekend,' the other man offered dryly.

This was his *king*. 'My apologies, Your Majesty. I was speaking to your sister.'

'I think we shall just turn up at this inn of yours to-morrow afternoon and take it from there. It'll add to the mystique. Ana says she'll bring Sophia, Silas and Lor, and clothes for us all, and will inform your apprentices and the horse master.'

'I appreciate it.' What else could he say? He was being given far more leeway than he deserved.

'Make her happy, Tomas. My sister deserves to be loved for exactly who she is. She's a remarkable woman. A unique treasure. I don't surrender her lightly.'

'Noted.'

'Several of my father's old guard politicians are try-ing to tear her down because of the progress she repre-sents, and they'll come for you as well. No more flying under the radar. You're going to be too close to the throne. They'll shred your reputation and try to ruin whatever you attempt to build. You need to learn to play the power game.'

'Not a problem.'

'One last question. Do you love her?'

What was love? He was attracted to Claudia beyond measure. He wanted to spend time with her, laugh with her, fight with her, and *be* that person she turned to in the darkness. He wanted to see her cradling his children, teaching them the names of the stars and mountains nearby. He would die before he let any harm befall her. No matter how unruly his feelings, they were fixed on her.

'I'm getting there,' he muttered. 'And, as you can imagine, it's quite the trip.'

CHAPTER NINE

THE TAVERN WAS clean and rustic and Tomas had liked it well enough when he'd stayed there before. Innkeeper Bain met them at the door several hours after midnight, sparing a swift glance for the sleepy, silent Claudia and a longer one for the eagle as he led them up the stairs and along a dimly lit corridor to the room Tomas had stayed in before.

'Fire's lit and we made up a couple of perches for your birds after last time. Don't know if they're the sort you usually use—Caitlin and Balo put their heads together and came up with them. You'd have thought they were making a throne, the time and care they put into it.' Pride laced his voice.

Tomas transferred Alhena to the tall, sturdy perch and removed the hood to let her survey her new surroundings. He'd put it back on soon enough, once he tethered her for the night. The bath pan below the perch was empty, but it was a nice touch.

'You know, if it's capital you need in order to bring in paid help in order to free Caitlin up so she can follow her dreams, I have it to spare. You're never going to lose her completely. She loves you and she's part of the fabric of this place. She could apprentice to me through the day, a four-day week even, I'd make that concession for her and for you, and she would return to you at night.'

'Has she asked this of you?'

'I asked her a general question about interviewing for an apprenticeship with me. She wouldn't even consider it. Said you needed her more.'

'Everyone has childhood dreams of becoming something fancy.'

'That they do, Innkeeper.' Claudia entered the conversation gently. 'You must be so proud of your daughter for the answer she gave my fiancé. I know I would be. And a little bit sad about that answer too.'

The man didn't seem to want to look at her. She had that effect on people sometimes, when she chose to cut straight to the heart of things.

'There's bread and cheese on the table, wine and water as well, and stew downstairs if you want it reheated. I wasn't sure,' he muttered.

Claudia shook her head, so Tomas answered for them both. He was hungry but not that hungry. 'Thank you, no. This is good.'

'You'll be wanting breakfast too, I suppose. Downstairs like before?'

'Up here,' said Claudia before Tomas could answer. 'Please.'

The innkeeper nodded and headed for the door. 'Think that's all.'

There was one other thing. 'We want to get married tomorrow,' Tomas told him. 'Are you available to perform the service?'

The grizzled older man turned back towards them but barely raised a brow. 'I need two weeks' notice to get the paperwork in order. It's the law.'

'The paperwork will be waived.'

'Never heard of that happening.'

'Trust me,' Tomas murmured. He had a king in his pocket. 'It can be done.'

'In that case, m'lord, I'm available.'

Claudia chose that moment to lower the hood of her dusky blue travelling cloak. The material was a coarse woollen weave, nothing special. Her face, however, could stop a man's breath. Unless Bain had been living under a rock lately, he would know who she was. 'Thank you, Innkeeper,' she murmured. 'I didn't catch your name.'

'Bain, m'la— Your Gr— Royal… Princess… *God*.'

Claudia smiled. 'That's quite an escalation, but don't worry about it. I'll write my name out in full for you for tomorrow.' She nodded towards Tomas. 'His too.'

Bain bowed and nodded at the same time. 'Thank you, Princess. I'm just going to…get you better wine.'

'Don't bother,' Tomas told him. 'You can expect a team of guards to roll in soon. They'll station themselves around the tavern tonight. You might want to warn people.'

Bain pulled out a set of old-fashioned door keys. 'Let me just make sure the *second bedroom* is open for your use.'

'Plausible deniability, how *thoughtful*,' murmured Claudia. 'Thank you so much. Your service is impeccable.'

'It would have been even *more* impeccable had we

known you were coming. Will any *other* guests be joining your wedding party tomorrow?'

'They will,' said Claudia smoothly. 'Discretion is required.'

He closed his eyes and ran his hand across his face.
Squinted at them from between his fingers before dropping his hands to his sides. 'You're still here.'

Tomas sighed. 'Yes.'

'Discretion it is.' Innkeeper Bain made it through the
door and shut it firmly behind him.

'We should marry here. At the inn,' declared Claudia.

'It's more of a tavern.' She hadn't seen the downstairs bar yet.

'It'll be a wedding venue before he knows it.'

Tomas couldn't help but smile. 'That's just cruel.'

She headed for the table and unwrapped a block of
hard cheese from within a waxy cloth and took a knife
to it. 'It's soft cheese I shouldn't be eating while pregnant.' She nibbled an edge. 'I think this is Cheddar.' She
slipped a slice between a bread roll and bit in, before
loosening her cloak and draping it over a chair by the
fire. 'This is a nice room. Lived in. Not quite as nice
as my tent, but acceptable.' She took another bite and
studied a faded painting on the wall.

She hadn't always lived as a princess. She didn't mind
taking her meals in Lor's kitchen. He needed to keep re-
minding himself of those facts or he'd go mad thinking
that she'd never be satisfied with his version of normal.
'I'm a plain man,' he warned.

'You're definitely not that plain. Possibly a little deluded, though.'

He tried again. 'I like plain things.'

Her mouth was full but her eyebrows spoke volumes.

'You, of course, are not plain at all,' he added quickly. 'What I mean is that I don't want to live a fancy life. A simple one will do, and I'm not sure that's going to suit you.'

She took her time swallowing her food. 'Because I'm a princess, and princesses can't live simply?'

'Yes.' Why did he feel as if he was eleven years old all over again, telling her she couldn't be a falconer? He'd been wrong about that. Maybe he could be wrong about this too.

'Have I been living lavishly at the fortress?' she asked. 'Redecorating? Insisting on formal dining? No. I eat in Lor's kitchen as often as you do.'

'And then there's your princess clothes,' he offered heavily. There was absolutely no arguing about those. 'Can I afford to keep you in clothes? I'm thinking no.'

'My official clothing requirements are covered by the Crown. All part of the job description for the Princess Royal. But when I come looking for you at the aviaries, how am I dressed?'

'Simply.' He had to admit that.

'And you haven't seen me of a morning lately. Be warned—my morning sickness is brutal. Why do you think I'm cramming this food down now? Because I'm practical and I like good plain food, a warm fire and a clean bed. I think it's time that you put your thoughts about us not sharing similar values behind you. Deal?'

'Done.' He took a deep breath and recommitted to the path he'd chosen for them both and dug for the inner strength and confidence required to walk it. 'So.' He shed his coat, emboldened by the way her gaze lowered to the snug fit of his trousers and his plain cotton shirt that did have a few buttons at the neck but otherwise pulled on and off like a T-shirt. Very plain. Possibly flattering, according to the sudden appreciation in her eyes. 'We have no nightwear.'

She arched one single elegant brow. 'Surely you have a spare shirt somewhere.'

Such a long way to go to the car and get his duffel and bring it in. 'No.'

'Well, then.' She removed her cloak and placed it over a nearby chair, and then set her socks and boots beside it. Tidy. Her embroidered shift followed and then her trousers. He didn't look away as she sauntered towards the bathroom. 'I think Alhena should sleep in the other room, don't you? Wouldn't want to disturb her.'

'I can sort that.'

'Will you be showering before bed too?'

'And then joining you in bed, naked. Yes.'

She slid him a brilliant smile. 'Perfect.'

Only when she'd disappeared from view did he put his hands to his face much as the innkeeper had done. She'd been outfoxing him from the moment she'd seen him again and he showed no signs whatsoever of gaining the upper hand. But he had a true heart, his course was set, and his bed skills had pleased her last time around. If he could keep his head in that regard, reduce her to a quivering wreck *first*, maybe there was hope for him.

He crossed to the eagle. 'I'm going to pick up your stand with you still on it and put you in the other room.

No protest, now, you'll like it. And tomorrow I'll take you downstairs and introduce you to Caitlin and Balo. You'll like that too.'

The eagle stayed quiet for him as he set her up in the adjoining room and tied her off. To call her an attack bird was doing her a disservice, given her placid nature. She'd been with him for over seven years and he'd been putting potential mates before her for the past three. She liked being around people too much to pay attention to any of that, though. Alhena the star had quite forgotten how to be a bird.

That or she was excessively picky. Emotionally un-available, much like he had once been, but look at him now. Getting married tomorrow and all that. Rushing in to stake his claim and protect, protect, *protect* what was his.

He was shirtless by the time he returned to the main bedroom. He was completely naked by the time he reached the shower cubicle.

Claudia smiled and moved aside to let him enter.

He took his place, every nerve alive and reaching.

And let the future in.

Claudia loved it when Tomas took charge. She needed him to take control in order to surrender. No more think-ing or planning or trying to stay one step ahead and be safe. She was *already safe* with this beautiful man, and with that came the freedom to follow wherever he led. She closed her eyes as the kiss they shared deepened, relearning the taste of him and the warm expertise of hungry lips. He lifted a hand to the back of her neck, his thumb below her jaw, the better to tilt her head, and there was a sensuality about him, a willingness to let pleasure rule, that left her flushed and breathless.

He took the soap from her and placed her hands on his chest. He soaped up his hands and started at her fingertips, and then the vee between her fingers. He circled her wrists and kissed her as he worked soap up her arms and over her shoulders. She shuddered into him when his hands cupped her breasts, gentled by slick suds as warm water rained down her back.

Her nipples pebbled for him, and it wasn't just because his skilled fingers were attentive. It was him. Her Tomas.

He turned her so she could lean back against him as he took the shower hose and directed it to remove the soap on her arms and breasts and then he moved the pressure lower, and between the water and his fingers coaxed her to swift orgasm.

'Cheat,' she murmured when she'd recovered breath to speak.

'I'll make it up to you.'

She took her leave a short time later while he got clean, but not before she let her gaze linger over his erection. 'That's for me, right?'

He gave himself a leisurely stroke, his eyes never leaving her face. 'Yes.'

'And you won't be long? Because all I'm going to do is be in bed trying to arrange my body to best advantage. That's going to drive me mad with indecision in *very* short order.'

She'd made him smile. Impossible not to feel smug about that.

'On your back, hands beneath the pillow.'

She could do that. 'And my legs?'

'Apart.'

But of course.

He put his face to the spray and she put her mind to drying off and pushing back the bedclothes. Wouldn't want to obstruct his view.

He took her to pieces all over again once he finally joined her. Generous with his tongue and touches in all the right places and when he finally entered her she could no longer keep her hands to herself, weaving them in his hair and putting all her joy and hopes for them into a kiss that brought tears to her eyes.

'I dreamed of you,' she murmured when he broke the kiss and rolled his hips and made her gasp. 'Soon as I saw you after all those years away, I started dreaming of being spread open beneath you and feeling so cherished.'

'Are you feeling cherished yet?' He set his lips to the tender skin of her neck and she was so close to orgasm she could almost reach the stars.

'I am.' And then he rolled her atop him and put the pad of his thumb to her centre and surged up into her with those strong, muscular thighs and she closed her eyes and surrendered. 'I'm feeling everything.'

When she clenched around him and stilled his hand and brought it to her stomach, he tumbled after her.

Mornings were hell. This was Claudia's reality. Not even a night of bliss and a soundly sleeping Tomas at her side could alter that reckoning. She slid from the bed and made it to the bathroom without retching but she was glad to shut the door behind her. She clung to the basin, head down and begging for her nausea to recede before glancing at her reflection in the mirror. Bird's nest dark hair, pale face, and redness on her neck where Tomas's facial hair had rasped her skin. He had no beard but he must have to shave every day. Soon she would know many such personal details.

Husband. She touched the extra colour around her nipples. He'd used her incredibly sensitive breasts to ruthless advantage last night and she'd loved every bit of it.

Father. Her father had not been a kind man. Tomas's father, for all his sternness and adherence to rules, had been patient, protective and kind, and Tomas would be too. He would be the kind of parent every child deserved. Her hand went to her still flat stomach. All she needed to concentrate on right now was bringing this baby safely into the world and being a decent wife to an honourable man who would never have chosen to marry her if not for the way she'd pushed.

'Work with it,' she whispered to her reflection. Hadn't that been her motto for all the long years she'd spent in exile? *Make it work for everyone involved.* She took a deep breath and stood up straighter and summoned a smile.

C'mon, Claudia, where are you? You don't have to be loved to be happy. You don't even have to be especially wanted as long as you're useful to have around. You can be useful, can't you? Just do it and don't think too much about what could have been. Just make the most of whatever you're given.

There you are, girl. Don't fail me now.

Claudia the unwanted child, the resourceful survivor, the woman who, for all her faults, had never hardened her heart against hope. Bravado too would see her through, because she had plenty of that. Bravado and hope.

'It's the best way forward for all of us,' she murmured and sealed the deal with a nod.

And promptly doubled over and lost the contents of her stomach.

By the time she poked her head around the bathroom door, Tomas was up and dressed and the fire was crackling in the hearth. His dark eyes searched her face, a frown between his eyes.

'I used the bathroom in the other room,' he said. 'How are you feeling?'

'I'm pretty good by mid-afternoon, but most mornings are a bit rough. Would you mind passing me my clothes?'

He moved gracefully for such a big man.

'They're bringing breakfast,' he said as he gathered up last night's clothes and gave them to her. 'I ordered everything.'

'I hope you're hungry enough for two then, because I'm making no promises when it comes to keeping anything down.'

'Is that normal?'

'Apparently.'

'Is there anything else you need?'

Where did she begin? This was her wedding day, after all.

'I can ask people to bring your belongings here. I can go and get them.'

'No!' She took a deep breath and promptly swallowed hard on a fresh wave of nausea. 'No leaving me.' And boy, was it going to take a world of therapy to unpack that little outburst. 'I can make do. We discussed this last night. I'll be out in a minute.'

She dressed quickly and braided her hair and made good on her promise to emerge from the bathroom. She'd only taken a few steps before there was a knock on the door and a cheerful girlish voice called out, 'Breakfast!'

What was the young woman's name again? Kaity? Catherine?

The girl breezed in when Tomas opened the door, carrying a laden tray piled high with food. 'Da said to make it an extra special tray. He even wanted me to pick flowers, but you try finding roses in the mountains at this time of year, and besi—' The young woman stopped abruptly, her lips forming a perfect O to match her startled eyes. She tried to curtsey, tray and all. The tray tilted and rattled alarmingly until Tomas rescued it and set it on the sideboard.

'Morning, Caitlin. Meet my fiancée.'

'Your—? That's the Princess Royal!' whispered Caitlin.

'And also my fiancée.'

Caitlin slid him a beseeching glance and nervously

smoothed her apron skirt. 'What are the words? What do I call her?'

'*Your Royal Highness* the first time you see her, and if you see her again the same day you call her *ma'am*.' He was quiet with his directions, no fuss, and it seemed to steady the young girl.

If Claudia hadn't already been besotted with him, his behaviour these past twenty-four hours would have made her so.

'Your Royal Highness, ma'am!'

'And now stand up,' murmured Tomas, and Claudia wanted to put the girl at ease too, the way Tomas had, but the rich smell of cooked sausage and bacon was her undoing. She barely managed a nod before bolting to the bathroom and starting with the stupid morning sickness all over again. It didn't matter to her brain or her stomach that there was nothing left to bring up. She would go through the motions anyway until her throat burned with the sour taste of stomach acid and she felt like a wrung-out rag.

An eon later, when she slid to her knees and leaned her head against her forearm on the toilet bowl, she saw a damp wash cloth dangling in front of her.

The hand holding the cloth didn't belong to the girl.

Tomas settled on the floor beside her and lifted her into his arms as if she weighed barely anything at all. She tucked her head beneath his chin, too embarrassed and grateful for words.

'I sent the breakfast away.'

'Thank you. The smell…'

'I figured.'

'She'll guess I'm pregnant.'

He made a humming noise that might have been agreement. 'Is that something you want to hide?'

'I'm undecided.' Part of her wanted everyone to know now that Tomas knew, so she could go about changing her life to fit the circumstances. Part of her knew her reputation would take a hammering and it would reflect badly on the royal family—best to get it over with. And then there was Tomas's reputation and new position to think of. 'Do you want me to pretend I'm not pregnant until we've been married a while?'

'I think we're past that.'

Who knew pragmatism could be so attractive?

'Let's just shape our lives and the life of our child to best advantage. No lies, we're just doing things our own way. Why *wouldn't* we marry with a baby on the way?' he continued.

'Do you really want to do this?' She was having second thoughts. That or her earlier thoughts were back to haunt her. 'You'll be trapped and resentful.'

'I'll be *grateful* and do everything in my power to prove my worth as a husband and father. You keep telling me I'm good enough to stand with you, so get out of my way and let me fight for us. I'm ready. Besides, I'm not the only one here whose life has been turned upside down.' His voice had grown gruff. 'Yours has been upended too. You get to bear this child, ready or not. You get me for a husband, whether you want me or not.'

'I'm ready.' Her love for the child growing in her belly was already a fierce and twisty force. 'I want it all. Anyone who says you're not good enough to stand at my side is going to get schooled on the many reasons why they're *wrong*. I'll slay all those demons and I'll *make* you a believer, see if I don't.'

'Funny. You don't *look* all that fierce, curled up here in my arms.'

The steady beat of his heart beneath her ear seemed like a good start. She closed her eyes and let herself relax. People thought she didn't have nerves or insecurities. Even her brother saw her as some kind of indestructible force and, right or wrong, she tried to live up to the hype.

'You know how we're talking about our insecurities…'

'I heard you talking about *mine*.'

Dry as dust, this man who'd soon be hers for life.

'I have some too. People think I'm strong and fierce because I want to make a difference in this world and I'm prepared to make enemies along the way,' she mumbled into the well-worn weave of his shirt. 'I know how to fight and wait and play the long game and win. And sometimes being that person is easy and sometimes I run on pure bravado. I need—' *you*, her helpful voice supplied, but she could be more specific, and less '—I would love to have someone who can lend me their strength when mine runs out. I'd weep with relief to know that you too will have our baby's best interests at heart. I can let go and know you'll do everything in your power to keep us safe. That's a gift I've *never* had before and I'll give it the respect it deserves.'

'I won't fail you.'

'I can be strong again. I *will* be. I won't always feel so low.' She closed her eyes and soaked up his warmth.

'And I'll never think less of you for saying you need me,' he murmured. 'Say it as often as you like. My insecurities will thank you.'

Good to know their insecurities were compatible.

A soft knock sounded at the door of the outer room. 'Ma'am and Lord Tomas? It's Caitlin. I have two mugs of weak tea with some slices of lemon and ginger on the side. I'll leave them outside the door and if you want them, good, and if you don't, I'll collect them later.'

Tomas rubbed his thumb over her shoulder in a gesture she found comforting. 'Shall I tell her to bring it in?'

Claudia nodded.

'Come through, Caitlin.'

Moments later, the girl was kneeling beside them in the bathroom. 'My ma used to swear by lemon and ginger tea for soothing the stomach. The tea is Mrs Lee's mountain blend. She's Balo's *nonna*. Balo's the man I'm going to marry, but he doesn't know that yet, so if you could keep it to yourself for another year or two while I grow up, I'd appreciate it. Is there anything you'd like *me* to keep to myself? Because I can. This old place sees its fair share of secrets. Da says not spilling any is as much a part of being an innkeeper as not spilling the drinks.'

Such earnest eyes.

'I can see why you want Caitlin for your falcons, Tomas.' Claudia leaned forward and added lemon and ginger to both mugs and picked one up before settling back against him and bringing the mug to her lips to take the tiniest sip.

'Speaking of...' Tomas had a gleam in his eyes. 'Caitlin, there's a golden eagle in the spare bedroom and a gauntlet on the bed. If you could take her downstairs and find a chair or another perch for her by the fire, I'd be grateful. She's well behaved and enjoys watching people moving about.'

'*Me?*'

'You.'

'And we need another suite of rooms for our guests this afternoon,' he continued.

'Da said we have incoming and to give them the best room we have, but you're in it.'

'Make this room up fresh and we'll move to another,' said Claudia. 'Let's aim to keep my brother in a good mood, hmm?'

Caitlin's eyes grew impossibly round. 'I—the King? And Queen *Ana*? Here? As in *today*?'

'For our wedding,' Tomas supplied gravely, and never again would she suspect him of not having the most sublime sense of humour. Caitlin was already on the move. 'I guess your Da *can* keep a secret. Don't forget the eagle. Her name's Alhena.'

Ten minutes later, Claudia was almost halfway through her tea and they'd moved from the bathroom floor to the armchairs by the fire. For a woman on the morning of her wedding day she felt delightfully unbothered by details. The only detail that mattered was to marry the right man, and he was on the phone to Ildris, inviting him to their wedding through gritted teeth because she'd asked him to. She smiled into her cup when she heard him take it upon himself to ask Ildris to bring Alya too.

His future wife obviously valued them, and they owed her, he said next.

Maybe he'd learn to be a little less heavy-handed when it came to wielding power or maybe he'd never get the hang of it. Claudia was looking forward to a lifetime of brutal honesty, absolute trust and fireworks, no matter what. A pox on emotional containment. It was overrated.

'What?' he asked as he ended the call and pocketed his phone. 'They'll be here mid-afternoon. I told them they might have to share a room if they were staying on.'

'So I heard. But, by my reckoning, Caitlin said there are six rooms in total, and if the King and Queen are in one, with Sophia in an adjoining room, Silas and Lor in another, and you and me in one, the count is only four rooms taken. Why would Ildris and Alya have to share a room?'

He smiled wickedly. 'Never said I could count.'

This man. This life stretching out ahead of them.

Savour the moment, Claudia. Those funny, fleeting, happiest of moments.

They'll sustain you.

CHAPTER TEN

TOMAS MADE HIS way downstairs the moment Cas and his entourage arrived, and he might have been driven to drink as a way of settling the nerves that had crept up on him but for the steadying presence of Rudolpho and horse master Gabriel, who'd also hitched a ride in one of the two royal helicopters now sitting in a field behind the inn. He knew these men and they knew him. He was happy to see them and took great pleasure in watching Balo's *nonna*—who'd been put in charge of the wedding flower arrangements—pin sprigs of flowering thyme and wild mountain heather to their shirts.

News of the wedding spread through the village with the arrival of those royal helicopters carrying the royal family. Far from this wedding being an impromptu and modest affair, the people of Aergoveny seemed hellbent on embracing their King, country and especially their new Lord, and making Tomas's wedding to the Crown Princess an evening to remember.

Tomas and his companions were herded to the outdoor fires where the men of the village had gathered, and music and dancing was already in full swing. Women walked past on their way to the inn, bearing armfuls of wild mountain flowers and baskets of food, and everyone shared wide smiles and teasing glances and embraced the festivities with a skip in their step.

Rudolpho and the village mayor had taken it upon themselves to form an alliance and see to it that Tomas met as many people as possible in the hours before the ceremony began. Gabriel harnessed the younger men and encouraged their most prized steeds to be brought to him immediately for examination. The King's wedding gift to the village included a year's access to royal racehorse bloodlines, he told them, and promptly turned the wedding gathering into a horse traders' paradise.

'Just making it a wedding to remember,' he said.

'My father grew up in a mountain village,' Rudolpho told Tomas a short time later as the men co-opted by the women to help with preparations began bringing out ornate soup tureens and tables. Tomas gratefully accepted a cup of strong hot coffee brought to him by the mayor's grandson.

People started turning up with their hawks and, well, what was a falconer to do in the face of that kind of temptation but set a prize of first pick from his next hatching and help set out a flight path for time trials?

Rudolpho, being a courtier well used to keeping wayward kings on task, warned Tomas not to get too involved, this being his wedding day and all, and then the women signalled they were ready for him, so he jostled his way to the head of the crowd, straightened his trousers and shirt and the stunning fur cloak Ildris had slung over his shoulders at some point, and made his way towards the village square, where his bride waited with her family.

At some point the small, intimate gathering Tomas had imagined had become a celebration for all, because how else would this place beneath the sky and in the shadow of a great mountain range have become ringed with mountain wildflowers and pine boughs, and made raucous with rhythmic clapping and spirited vocals? With his blood quickening and his gaze searching ahead for that moment when Claudia would be revealed to him, he gave himself over to the moment, cupped his hands over his mouth and let out a piercing war cry of his own.

He didn't even have a gift to lay at her feet—he really hadn't thought this marriage moment through. And then he saw her and the air around him stilled and the music faded to nothing.

She wore a royal tiara and a simple white gown and a fur-trimmed cloak similar to his, and she smiled at him as if there were no other place she'd rather be than here with him.

He led an army of Aergovenich warriors, young and old, who would follow his lead, and he didn't know when he'd become their figurehead but they put the weight of their wedding songs and customs and posturing behind him and it was glorious.

Bain the innkeeper stopped him from reaching Claudia's side by the simple act of getting in his way and holding his ground until they stood chest to chest.

At the raising of Bain's hand, all sound stopped.

'Crown Princess Claudia of Byzenmaach, is this him?'

'It is.'

'King Casimir of Byzenmaach, do you consent to placing your treasured sister, the country's beloved Crown Princess Royal, into this man's hands?'

'If she insists, yes.'

'Lord Ildris of the mountain clans, do you object to the placing of your beloved jewel of the north into this working man's hands?'

'I dare not object.'

'Lord Falcon Master Sokolov, are you worthy of this beloved woman?' roared Bain at his most formidable volume yet.

Tomas realised why Bain had so suddenly developed a taste for theatre when the army of men behind him bellowed, 'Yes!' until Tomas raised his hand for silence.

The resulting hush nearly stole his breath.

And then Lor stepped up. He hadn't expected her to play a prominent role in the ceremony, but nothing so far had proceeded as expected and her kindly face was reassuring.

'Tomas Sokolov, you were born in my presence and, as you stand here before me, I claim my role as representative of the spirit of your parents. Do you object?'

'No.' He probably should have gone over the details of this wedding in advance…

'Your future wife stands before you and us all,' continued Lor. 'And, as is customary, I demand you open your heart for examination.'

Did she want him to cut it out? This might shorten his life span considerably, which might even please Cas and Ildris. Cas was smiling broadly and Ildris looked annoyingly pleased with himself. Neither seemed to want to clue him in on his options regarding this particular part of the ceremony. Then again, he'd winged it so far.

'I have nothing to hide,' he offered grandly.

Although a little bit of mystique when it came to lording it over the people of Aergoveny might have come in handy.

'Will you honour her?' Bain asked.

'Yes.' The answer was his alone, but no less compelling than the hundreds of voices that had gone before.

'Will you cherish her?'

'Beyond measure.'

'Will you protect her from harm?'

'With my life.'

Lor smiled proudly. How much more was there to go? 'Do you love her?'

There was such hope in her eyes and a faint plea not to embarrass her by saying something ridiculous like 'No' or 'I might' or 'We'll see'. That time had passed.

'I love her with every breath I take, yes.' And probably beyond, but no one had asked for that.

Yet.

Lor turned to Claudia, who stood tall and still, eyes shining. 'Princess Claudia of Byzenmaach, Lady Falconer of the North, he is worthy and he is yours. Will you have him?'

Claudia stepped up close and trailed a finger around his jaw, tilting his face first to one side and then the other. She was enjoying this horse-trading segment just a little too much. She strolled a leisurely circle around him, measuring the breadth of his shoulders with her fingers and the strength of his patience while he awaited her answer and his army looked on.

'Yes.'

And the celebrations began in earnest.

'I can't believe you didn't have to say any of the vows,' he muttered hours later in the privacy of the tavern's second-best bedroom. The room had been lit with so many candles, he figured the Vatican must surely be missing some. And Claudia sat in a chair with her hair down, her feet up and her tiara on the table while the celebrations continued elsewhere.

She looked tired but gratifyingly content. He, on the other hand, rubbed at the place where his heart used to be, firmly convinced that she'd picked it up and put it somewhere with casual abandon. It was probably underneath that priceless diamond and sapphire tiara on the table.

'I still don't believe that there I was, lying prostrate at your feet...'

'Figuratively speaking,' she said airily, with a languid wave of her hand.

'Pledging my all for eternity...'

'Or face a public hanging, I did like that bit.'

He'd always suspected she was the bloodthirsty sort.

'And all you had to do was say, *He'll do, thanks. Yes.*'

'You're the one who thought an Aergoveny village wedding would be a cinch. I mean, who knew they'd make you their essence of masculinity for the day? That looked fun. Was that fun?'

Maybe if he'd known what he was doing...

'I thought you represented them *very* pleasingly. I counted at least three new unions to come of it.'

'Please tell me Caitlin didn't corner Balo.'

'Not yet. Her father knows her heart and so does Balo. It will happen in time, but not yet.'

'Alya and Ildris?'

'I saw them leaving together arm in arm,' she murmured.

'Ha.' His gaze flew to Claudia's stomach. 'How are you feeling?'

'Married.'

'Good, because I'm only ever going to do that once. How is our baby feeling?'

She'd closed her eyes but cracked one open, just a slit. 'Too small to tell, but I think it's all good. Tomorrow morning will be a repeat of this morning, but with more cake involved. I did eat a lot of cake. The vanilla frosting was on point.'

Where had the people come up with enough food to feed and water six hundred at such short notice? And they were still going, those wedding celebrations, and somehow, he was going to have to make good on those vows he'd made before everyone and God.

'I'm sorry you had to lie about loving me. I know you don't. Not really.' She had her eyes closed again, so missed his double-take. He opened his mouth to tell her that although he'd been put ruthlessly on the spot in full public view, he hadn't been lying when he'd made those vows. He'd meant every word.

How could she not have recognised his sincerity?

Even if he had just been grumbling about the uneven-
ness of their vows.

'I—'

But she was already speaking again, her voice coming
in over his. 'I want you to know that I'm going to do everything I possibly can to make this union work. I don't
want to disappoint you. I'm determined to be of use.'

Of use.

She was *of use* to her brother.

She'd been *of use* to Ildris and his ilk.

Why was being of use so important to her sense of
self? Was she really so motivated by service to others
or had it merely been a survival tactic for far too many
years?

He hesitated before speaking his mind, not quite
knowing how his next words would be received. 'You
have a thing about being useful to others. You turn
yourself inside out for people and put their needs above
yours, but that's not how I want this marriage to work.
You don't exist to be used by others. Let's figure out
together what moving forward means, and go easy on
the one-way self-sacrifice.'

She put the heels of her hands to her eyes as if his
words hurt her. His heart ached for her.

'For example,' he continued doggedly. 'You've talked
about not feeling at home in the places you live. Should
creating a home base where we feel completely and utterly ourselves be our number one priority?'

'Yes.' It sounded like a sob, but it was a yes.

'Could a modest manor house in the middle of nowhere, with no old memories attached, ever become such a place for you?'

'Yes.'

'Clean slate. New beginnings. A baby on the way. We can make new memories. Beautiful ones. No matter what has brought us to this moment, will you do that with me, and *for* me, and, most importantly, for yourself?'

'Yes.'

'Good.' He pulled her into his arms and she curled into him and clung as if she'd never let him go. 'It's not so bad, this being married business,' he declared gruffly. 'We're going to nail this.'

CHAPTER ELEVEN

BEING MARRIED HADN'T actually changed his way of life all that much, decided Tomas several months later. He'd known from the beginning not to expect Claudia to be a stay-at-home wife, eagerly awaiting his return after a day of blissful homemaking, but the time she spent in service to the Crown and the various charities she'd adopted, and her continued service to Ildris and his northerners, meant she didn't actually spend a lot of time in Aergoveny.

Likewise, he was busier than ever as he travelled between the manor and the winter fortress and carved out the time to join his princess wife at the various state banquets and luncheons Casimir insisted they attended.

Far from his reputation being sullied, it had been thoroughly gilded once his high-country wedding to the Crown Princess had become common knowledge. The people of Byzenmaach approved of Claudia's choice of partner. Photos of him and his eagles had helped. He was of Byzenmaach and his pedigree went back generations. He brooded photogenically.

He was the new Lord of Aergoveny, and Aergoveny had claimed him.

As Casimir had warned, he now had his own political capital to spend.

It had only taken one excruciatingly boring state dinner and a round of idle conversation between him and some of the courtiers who'd been stirring up rumours about Claudia's legitimacy and planting stories about her unfortunate Stockholm Syndrome. They'd even begun wondering aloud, and in his presence, when Claudia might give birth. Apparently, they'd thought themselves beyond reproach or justified in their smear campaigns. Perhaps they'd thought him toothless.

How deluded was that?

He'd begun by reminiscing about a particular hunting party some of them had attended at the winter fortress many years ago under the rule of the late Leonidas. Pity about those heinous rumours of sexual assault on the son of the Duke of Laire, wasn't it? Such a tragedy, the boy's subsequent suicide. Such a shame no one in attendance had ever seemed to have the stomach to get to the bottom of it.

Wasn't it?

So many stories of those dark times towards the end of King Leonidas's life.

Weren't there?

Claudia had called it extortion, or was it intimidation? One of those big words suggesting borderline criminal behaviour.

Tomas called it small talk.

They shared a bed once or twice a week—enthusiastically, he had no complaints—but as their baby grew, his touches became more tentative. There was a baby

in there! What was a man to do but be very, very careful in his approach?

He spent hours of every day setting up the new falconry the way he wanted it, and Claudia spent almost
every waking moment deep within the political bowels
of her brother's court, buying into the crisis of the day.
And there was always one of those.

He was everywhere and nowhere, always playing a
part these days. Only in the sanctuary of Lor's kitchen
did he allow himself to drop the mask and be himself
again. Claudia's wolfhounds were at his feet more often
than not, and he always had at least one falcon with him.
Sometimes Ana and Sophia would likewise find refuge
from the demands of the Crown while Claudia and Cas
debated policy and execution late into the night.

He might have even been content with his marriage
of—what had they called it?—two spirited individuals,
if he didn't already carry with him the memory of what
a loving marriage could be.

His parents had shown him the sweetness of silences
that did not clamour to be filled.

The intimacy of private glances and perfect understanding. The cups of tea in the morning, made with
care by a loving hand and served in a favourite mug.
Foundation memories. He wanted them.

His morning coffee whenever he stayed in Claudia's
suite at the palace came on a silver tray at exactly seven
a.m., lukewarm, too weak and utterly impersonal. Just
this morning he'd barked at a maid who'd entered their
bedroom just as he'd exited the shower. He hadn't expected her to be there.

He hadn't liked the way her sly sideways gaze had flicked at him.

'Did you really need to send her away so curtly?' Claudia had chided.

'Did she really need to freshen the linen at five minutes past six in the morning?' he'd snapped back.

He hated losing control of his responses and being found lacking.

And for all their fine talk about making a home for themselves and loving memories to go with it, neither he nor Claudia were making that happen.

Lor took that moment to place a hot mug of beef broth on the table in front of him and although he said his thanks, he promptly got lost in the thought that Claudia wouldn't even know it was *his* mug, let alone that he'd made it at school one year and given it to his mother as a birthday gift. The last time Claudia had set a cup of anything down beside him… Nope, she never had.

Lor, Ana and young Sophia all knew more about him than his wife did.

And off he went, being morose again.

This right here was why letting emotions rule your life was a *bad* thing.

And then Sophia clambered up on the stool next to him, bringing her special soup in her special cup with her, and regarded him solemnly. 'Did one of your falcons die?'

'No.' He certainly hoped not. Sophia's fixation with death was well known, mainly because she'd been told from a young age that both her father and aunt were dead when they weren't.

'Did you make a mistake and get into trouble?'

'Maybe.' He huffed a laugh. 'Why?'

'You're sad.'

'Nah.' He held up his forefinger and thumb, set approximately an inch apart. 'Maybe this sad. I was thinking about my mother, who died a long time ago. I made this mug for her when I was about as old as you are now. Have you done mug making yet?'

She shook her head with vigour. That would be a no, then. 'But I want to.'

'And you will,' said Ana. 'Say goodnight, Sophia. It's bedtime for you and me.'

Everyone in the kitchen began the goodnight chorus and by the time the heavy kitchen door swung shut, Tomas was halfway through his soup and determined not to look sad again, even if he was.

'Are you happy about becoming a father soon?' asked Lor with far more of a read on him than he was comfortable with.

'Sophia's a nice kid. I like kids.' Which didn't exactly answer the question. 'Raising a kid who's a member of the royal family to have similar values to the ones I grew up with won't be easy, though.' First time he'd voiced that thought. 'How do you teach someone to value a misshapen mug when they have access to the best of everything? Does Claudia possess anything belonging to her mother, other than royal jewels? I don't think so.'

'Maybe not, but in my experience it pays to think of Claudia more as an orphan raised by a foster family. She's not going to let on that a particular possession of hers is important, even if it is. She may say some of the falcons are hers but there's no loyalty from them in return—she knows that just as well as you do. She has a horse she treasures, but it's cared for and ridden by Gabriel and his grooms these days because of her pregnancy. She does have two very loyal wolfhounds.'

They both looked down. Those wolfhounds were currently sitting at Tomas's feet.

He hadn't meant to take them on, but Claudia's palace meetings ran for days sometimes, whereas with him at least the dogs got a run.

Lor wiped her hands on her apron. 'Has she talked about their defection to you?'

'I didn't realise it was a competition.' But what if Claudia thought of it as such? 'I thought I was helping.'

'You are very caring, very competent and very helpful, yes. You bring rules and safety with you—I predict that your children will idolise you. But with that happy head start into parenting comes a warning. Don't cut your wife out of the child-raising if she doesn't take to it as naturally as you do. That woman has been surplus to requirements all her life. *Include* her. Make her feel essential to your wellbeing and happiness. *Talk* to her about what you want from this new world the two of you are creating. There is her northern world, to which she is beholden for keeping her alive. There is her brother's world, into which she brings challenge and reform—a world where she's more often cast as a villain so that Casimir can be seen as the good King. And then there's *your* world, and to my old eyes she's doing her damnedest to make you happy. It doesn't help that you disappear for days on end, leaving her to get on with paying her dues.'

'She wants me to go,' he protested. 'She encourages me to get on with paying mine.'

'And in a secure relationship, individually working hard and coming together when the work is done would be enough. Is your relationship secure, my stalwart heart? Or is there still so much to learn about each other and discuss? Can't do that when you spend most of your time apart.'

Who knew that having Lor point out the obvious could make him feel so miserably unfit for the role of husband?

'She comes in here some nights when you're away and without fail she reaches for your mug, and she treats it with the same care you do, even though she doesn't know its history. She just knows it's yours.' Lor eyed him shrewdly. 'It's the little things that reveal so much, isn't it. Who you really are. What you value most. Even if you don't know how to keep hold of it.'

'Keep talking.' Might as well admit he needed some tough love. 'I don't know what I'm doing wrong, but my marriage is withering.'

'You need my wise words.'

Yes, he did. 'I need to fix it.'

'Claudia doesn't want to let anyone down and they use her and you know this. She'll work herself to the bone in service to others, it's happening in front of your eyes. She finds it very difficult to even state her wants and needs, let alone follow through. So get in there and put your foot down, Tomas, and make it easier for her to follow through.'

He was listening.

Two days later, Tomas braved the underground swimming pools of the winter fortress in search of his princess wife. He didn't like the watery caverns carved into the side of the mountain, no matter how many sconces lit his way. He didn't see luxury in the fluffy towels and scented oils placed strategically. He found the place eerie, truth be told. Give him sky above his head, not solid rock all around him. Maybe he just wasn't a cave person.

But Silas said Claudia had taken to bathing here of an afternoon, so he swallowed his dislike and journeyed forth, into the gloom.

Claudia sat by herself beneath the waterfall, a wrap tied around her rapidly changing body, her head slightly forward to let the water from the underground riverway pound down on her shoulders and neck.

By the time he'd removed his clothes she'd seen him and had made her way to the shallow end of the pool where the steps were, her amber eyes alight with curiosity and…dare he imagine pleasure?

'I thought you were away for two more days,' she said by way of greeting.

'I heard from Lor that your meeting was cancelled, so I asked Balo's grandfather to step in and supervise the apprentices through to the beginning of next week. Might work, might not. Delegation is not my strong point, but I'm trying to build teams that won't fall apart in my absence.'

'He must be good for you to even consider bringing him on.'

'He reminds me of my grandfather.' Tomas settled on the step beside her, half in the water, half out. 'He handles the goldens in ways I've never seen before, but it works. I can learn from him. That region is a treasure trove. Have I thanked you for choosing it for me lately?'

'Not lately.'

He leaned in and captured her lips in a kiss that started gently and then he very deliberately set about adding layer after layer of gossamer passion and promise.

'Thank you,' he whispered when his body had stirred sufficiently to make it abundantly obvious that he was pleased to see her. 'I can't wait to get you there more often. Did I tell you that Caitlin's father has taken on a new manager? I interviewed her for an apprenticeship yesterday.'

'Really?' Delight looked good on her.

'I offered her the position on the spot. It's people, isn't it. Key people in key positions who can change the world. She's one of them. You're one of them too.'

She smiled and leaned against him and it was enough to make him happy.

'I like it when you touch me or lean against me or trail your hand across my shoulders when you walk by,' he rumbled, mindful of Lor's advice that he should be more forthcoming. He was getting used to having to use his words more in all sorts of situations, rather than expect others to pick up on his non-verbal cues.

'You like it when I scratch the feathers at the back of your neck too.'

He huffed a laugh. So he did. 'Blame it on my early childhood conditioning. My father was a man of gestures rather than words. When I was younger, he'd carry me on his shoulders. When I got older I'd work my skinny little kid guts out to earn a pat on the back. My mother was big on putting my favourite food in front of me in my favourite bowl. Then she'd run her hand through my hair and mutter about there being more twigs in it than a bird's nest.'

'So touch is an expression of love for you. Good to know.'

'And you work yourself to the bone for the people you love. It's what you do. Baked into your psyche. It's what I want to talk to you about.'

She eyed him warily.

'You're doing too much for others and too little for us.' He came right out and said it.

She was silent a long time. Long enough for him to immerse himself in the water completely and rise, shaking the droplets from his hair and pushing the hair from his face. Hardly Aquaman, but she always seemed pleased enough with his body and that in turn pleased him.

'They need me.'

'They can't always have you. I and our baby are going to need you more.'

She dropped her gaze and skimmed her hands

through the water in lazy figure eights, making ripples but not splashes. A turbulence that lapped at his skin rather than attacked it.

'One of my ways of showing love as a kid was to try and be as invisible and unobtrusive as possible,' she offered finally. 'If I could just be still enough and silent enough, they could pretend I wasn't there, and Cas wouldn't have to try and protect me and end up taking a beating. Not breathing too loud was my version of love.'

And that was just heartbreaking, but he should have guessed. He'd seen first-hand what her childhood had been like, never mind that she'd never been like that with him as a kid.

'Was it like that for you in the north as well?' He moved closer, putting his hands to her belly, and measuring growth in finger spans.

'To start with, yes. I breathed very quietly and I was always wondering where I would go or what I would do if they simply packed up and left me behind. Then I overheard one of the elders saying I'd be of more use once my father was dead and Cas became King and I clung to the thought that somehow I could be of use. I tried to learn as much as I could. I was forever putting myself forward, being the first to volunteer for anything and everything so I could *be of use.*'

'They manipulated you. I'll never think differently. But more to the point, don't you think you've repaid that debt in full?'

'I—don't know.'

'Ask them what more they want from you. Tell them your focus is shifting to your baby and allocate what you do for them to other people for the next six months. When they prove competent—and they will—leave them in those positions.'

He sneaked a glance and could see she was thinking it over as she chewed delicately on her bottom lip. Her matter-of-fact recounting of that time in her life horrified him. It sat at odds with how she usually spoke well of her time in the north. Maybe both versions could be true. Maybe all that mattered was that he understood her duality and listened to her concerns.

'It makes sense that you would swing from being barely visible to being all up in the thick of things, determined to be useful.' He pressed his lips to her belly. 'It makes sense that you're struggling to find a middle ground to reside in, but I'm here to help you find that balance if you'll let me. You are half a fingernail wider across the belly,' he declared.

'You think I'm failing you and our baby.'

'No,' he countered firmly. '*No*. But I want us to remember what we talked about on the night of our wedding and that we chose to make our relationship, our baby and our home, our first priority. And we haven't been, so let's do a reset. Both of us. Okay? I've been just as guilty as you of letting other things get in the way.'

He gathered her close and she clung to him. He hugged her tight and bobbed them up and down, dunking them at one point to wash away her tears. He cast about for something to show how deeply he wanted to make her feel wanted and secure.

'Balo's *nonna*'s a potter, so I made you a mug when

I went to see them about his grandfather stepping into that supervisory role.'

'You went to offer a man a job and ended up making a teacup?' Her smile was watery, but she wasn't crying that he could tell.

'Yes. It's wobbly but I think I've improved since I made that one for my mother—you'd recognise that one. It's the one in Lor's kitchen that I always use. I couldn't decide on a colour for your glaze—it's a toss-up between the blue of the sky or amber like your eyes. I have to go back to paint it once it's dry.'

'Blue. Blue for the sky.'

'You could come too and see what you think of the blue tableware for our day-to-day use at the manor. I liked it.'

She pulled away as far as he would let her—which wasn't far. 'Tomas Sokolov, are you *nesting*?'

'Is that what you call it?'

'What do you call it?' she demanded.

'I'd rather not think about my newfound fascination for pottery at all, but I do want you to come to Aergoveny with me tomorrow and stay the night if you have the time. The wolfhounds have missed you.'

'That's a lie. They miss their nomadic way of life. At least with you they get to ride out every now and then.'

'It's not a lie—I stand by what I said. They miss your company. So do I.' Words, words, using all the words until he broke through to her. She wasn't the only one who could learn new tricks. 'Please, I need you to take some time for yourself. We could ride out and explore. What did the doctor say about you riding?'

'Not to,' she replied dryly. 'I'm allowed to swim, so here I am, lolling about in the shallows because Cas has forbidden me to jump in the river opening, even though he still does.'

Tomas had been in that fast-flowing coil of darkness only once. Between the swiftly moving undertow and the grate at the end that could pin a person like a fly on a swat, he'd been fearful for his life. 'To be fair, it's a death trap.'

'Exactly. So Cas is now banned from swimming there too. He can't die until he and Ana have offspring that are old enough to sit on the throne without me having to be Regent. And you're not to take any notice of the rumour going around that I tried to poison my brother yesterday. That is not in my wheelhouse.'

'So…ah…what *did* happen to the King yesterday?' He dreaded the thought that Claudia would ever have to take her brother's place, but it could happen. She was next in line. Sophia hadn't been born in wedlock, so would never rule Byzenmaach. Royal succession rules were archaic and absolute.

'He got a stomach bug from Sophia, who got it from school. But don't let that get in the way of a good royal poisoning plot. Some courtiers work tirelessly to plant a wedge between me and Cas.'

'Who? I want names.'

'You can't have names if all you're going to do is threaten to reveal all their dark secrets if they oppose me.'

'Says who?'

'Says me.'

'Spoilsport. Claudia, listen to me. No one is ever going to come between you and your brother. The bond you forged in childhood grows stronger by the day. He needs and wants you in his life because he loves you. That you choose to support him so thoroughly is a blessing in his life, but you could step back tomorrow and he would still love you just the same. Talk to him about taking more time for yourself. Blame the baby, or me, but talk to him about placing your political focus where he needs it most and delegate the rest. You don't have a royal secretary—why not? Ask Rudolpho to train one and then *delegate*. You'll get more done in less time. I'm sharing my newfound wisdom with you freely so that you too may learn what I'm learning.'

'You're a saint.'

'Hardly. I just want more of you to myself.'

'Why didn't you just say you were feeling neglected?'

'Wouldn't have learned nearly as much about you if I'd come straight out and said it, now, would I?'

'You're *sneaky*.' She sounded delighted with that discovery.

'No, I'm not. I'm honest to a fault. And stalwart.'

'And naked.'

He hadn't forgotten. 'Have I mentioned how very pleased I am to see you?'

'Well, you have now.' She locked her legs firmly around his waist and began to rub herself against him. 'But I know how much you prefer nonverbal communication. Maybe you could show me.'

Challenge accepted.

CHAPTER TWELVE

KING CASIMIR AND Lord Ildris were negotiating. They'd been at it for hours and Claudia's interest had long since dwindled to nothing. The chairs around the negotiating table were outrageously comfortable but her lower back ached regardless. They kept calling for coffee refills for their tiny ceremonial coffee cups, but she'd stuck to water throughout the day, so not only was she not buzzing with caffeine, she'd had four toilet breaks in the past two hours.

Each time she excused herself the two men would stand and break the meeting until she returned, before once more getting down to business without her needing to say a word.

She'd spent two glorious days beforehand with Tomas at the manor that was fast becoming her favourite place in the world. They'd discovered a storeroom stacked with floor rugs, at which point Claudia had also discovered that an afternoon spent lounging on a sunny window seat stuffed with cushions while her husband and several of his apprentices revealed carpet after carpet for her to choose from was an excellent way to pass the time. Especially when said apprentices brought their falcons with them for socialising.

Returning to the palace so soon after watching Tomas effortlessly train and entertain and retain his authority throughout... Surely, she could be forgiven for thinking this high-level politicking a comedown from glorious heights?

As far as she could tell, her brother and Ildris were in agreement for the most part of this extended water use negotiation and were now haggling over minor details. Of course, those minor details weren't minor at all to the people who were affected by them, but she'd long since lost interest in the earnings projections of the Sorl River salmon farmers versus the hopes of the orchardists further downriver. She'd lost track of the many pros and cons of each five hours ago, which was around about the last time she'd made any meaningful contribution to the discussion.

Ildris was a good leader. So was her brother. Byzenmaach did not stand on the precipice of civil unrest and nor was it warmongering against its neighbours.

Could it be that these two men simply enjoyed talking decisions to death? More power to them, if that was their jam, but, well...

Did she really have to be here?

She stood and stretched, her hand on her lower back, which pushed her stomach out—and while she wasn't huge, there was no mistaking her these days for anything but well along in her pregnancy. Cas's eyes flashed from irritation to concern as he too rose from his chair.

The ever-present Rudolpho pulled her chair back as Ildris rose too.

'Again?' asked her brother.

'Again,' she murmured just a little too cheerfully. 'Your Majesty, Lord Ildris, I must beg your leave. My mind wanders, my back aches, and we're down to discussing minutiae. You don't need me here. That's a compliment, not a complaint.'

Ildris remained impassive, her brother frowned.

She wasn't above wondering if she should put her hand on her belly to further emphasise her need to be elsewhere, but that was guaranteed to make her brother frown more.

Cas's eyes narrowed as if reading her mind. 'Do you need to see your physician?'

'Only if I want her to tell me—again—that it's perfectly normal for pregnant women to have aching backs and get tired and go to the bathroom a lot.'

Rudolpho, bless him, was already opening the outer door for her.

'You'll be here tomorrow?' It was Cas her brother and not Cas her King asking. She was almost sure of it.

'No, I'm heading back to the mountains for the weekend. I want to be there when Tomas's black-necked and red-necked grebe pairs arrive.'

'His what?'

'Ducks.' She winked at Rudolpho. 'Yes, the sexiest falconer in the world collects endangered waterfowl and I am there for it.'

'Are these my ducks or his ducks?' Cas called after her. 'When did I agree to become king of the ducks?'

'You didn't. They're not yours. They're ducks of the world.' A playful Cas was an absolute delight. He didn't let himself go there nearly often enough. 'You're welcome!'

With her priorities rebalanced and Tomas more often by her side, Claudia began to spread her time more evenly between the royal palace, the fortress and the manor. She'd loved the Aergoveny manor house from afar and the reality did not disappoint. It had the potential to reflect the best of all her worlds and it suited Tomas to perfection. He had vision, natural authority, rock-solid steadiness and fairness at his command, and people responded by working hard for him. Falcons and learning and research and renewal of resources long forgotten. Why wouldn't people gladly follow him to the top of the world and back?

She was just over seven months pregnant now and last week the palace had released a statement saying she and Tomas were eagerly expecting their firstborn in November. Yes, people could count and would know that she'd been pregnant before marriage. Who cared?

Her life balance was better than good; it was amazing. Happiness had never been so easy to find.

Until the night Claudia stood alone in her dressing room in her brother's palace as she readied herself for yet another long afternoon of political jockeying disguised as small talk and noticed blood on her panties. Not a lot of blood. A few spots. Four. Maybe six spots overall, none of them big. But the blood was a bright, vibrant red and it rocked her confidence and put a fear in her that nothing else ever had.

She couldn't lose this baby.

Tomas would have no reason to stay with her if she lost the baby, no reason at all, and *no*. This wasn't happening. She wouldn't run, she'd just sit down, but not on a chair where the blood would soak in, and not on any carpet either. Just for a moment, she'd sit down on the floor in the bathroom, or lie down, that was better, and put her feet up on the edge of the bath and everything would right itself and there would be no problem at all.

She cradled her belly with tender hands. She didn't want to think about what might happen if there was no November baby for her and Tomas, Lord and Lady Sokolov of Aergoveny.

Would his vows stay true in the face of all that gaping nothing?

Who in her life had ever stuck around if she didn't deliver what they wanted?

'It's just your insecurities talking,' she told herself between jagged, too-loud breathing. 'Tomas's regard for you is real. You know this. He shows it every day.' He wasn't a man of love poems and verbal declarations of undying devotion. Actions counted more. He was committed to her and this life they were building. That wouldn't change. He was not a shallow man, this man she'd chosen. Loss might even bring them closer.

But later that night, after she'd begged off her meeting due to feeling unwell and had seen the doctor, who'd ordered more rest and fewer engagements…much later, after she'd returned to the winter fortress and taken herself to bed early, she didn't tell Tomas about those seven, eight, bright little spots on her panties. She pretended to be drowsy, already half asleep, and let him hold her, just hold her, as he drifted off to sleep.

While bits of her bled and she remained stubbornly, fearfully silent.

If she didn't say it, it wasn't happening.

Claudia took it easy the next day and the day after that.

She slept late and cancelled so many appointments that Rudolpho turned up, demanding to know what was happening.

The bleeding had stopped but fear kept her cautious, and she should have mentioned her spotting to Tomas before he left for Aergoveny for three days without her. She'd told him to go alone when he'd floated the idea of her going with him. She could tell he'd noticed her uncharacteristic need to sleep late and read quietly in her rooms of an afternoon. She wasn't walking her wolf-hounds or taking care of her falcons. Even in the most vicious throes of morning sickness, she'd always managed to do those things if she was within doing distance of them.

But pregnant women were not questioned when their habits changed abruptly, she'd come to notice.

At least, not by men.

Rudolpho being the exception, and that was only because he answered to the King.

'I have to tell him something,' Rudolpho emphasised for perhaps the hundredth time since he'd requested an audience with her. 'When is your current incapacity likely to end?'

'I don't know,' she told him tersely, not to mention truthfully. 'I don't feel up to sitting through a state luncheon today.'

'Have you seen your doctor? What did they say?'

'They told me to rest, so here I am. Resting.' The edge to her voice didn't go unnoticed. She stood abruptly, unable to stay still. 'I realise Cas is relying on me to help win over his senior courtiers to this new change to the water distribution plan, but the deal is done. They can whine all they want but the kings of four interlocked kingdoms are making this happen. Cas's old guard are just going to have to get over their vapours or be *replaced*.'

'Princess—'

'Don't you agree? It's time he stopped indulging them.'

'Quite, but—'

'It really is that simple. He. Is. Their. King. His word is *final*!'

Rudolpho was standing in front of her now, his dark eyes flashing concern. 'Your Highness, *please* sit down.'

'Stand up, sit down, come to lunch—what is it you all want from me?' Couldn't she even have a proper meltdown without someone trying to guide her through it?

'Princess, sit *down*.' The crack of a whip in his voice broke through her indignation. 'Let's not be alarmed, but ma'am, you're bleeding, and this concerns me *greatly*.'

She did as he said, sitting on the bed at first, and

then lying down as a cramp in her stomach struck hard. 'Don't tell Tomas.'

'Why in the world not?' He was already at the door to her suite, gesturing to someone outside. 'Find former housemistress Lor and bring her here. You, call the royal doctor and ask her to come urgently. *As in now, man, don't just stand there.*' He closed the door and turned back to Claudia. 'Feet up. Don't move.'

She closed her eyes on his forbidding frown. 'Please don't tell Tomas. He'll leave me if there's no baby to stay for.'

'Now I know you're out of your bleeding mind. No. No, brain bleeding at all,' he amended quickly. 'Out of your clearly addled mind. What have you been eating or drinking of late? Is there any chance you might have been poisoned?' She felt a smooth palm on her forehead. 'You're burning up. What about any unguents or skin potions? Have you used anything new?'

'Bath oil. I've been soaking in it. Bergamot and rose and…other smells. Lady Ester gave it to me.'

'Your late uncle's bitter mistress, who hated both your parents with a viciousness even I found impressive, gives you a gift and you didn't think to have it checked?'

Well, when he put it like that…

'Wait? Was Lady Ester my father's mistress? You tell me this now?'

'Your uncle's mistress.'

'Who was in all likelihood my—wait, do you know?' Was it her stomach or lower down? Hard to tell with the stabbing headache that had so recently arrived. 'No, you don't know *that* secret. No one does. Doesn't matter. Let it go. Shh. Keep trying to make me feel better instead.'

'How do you suggest I do that? You're burning up, I'm quizzing you about poisons, and your nose is bleeding.'

'My nose?' Her hand came up to examine it. 'Yes?' There was blood on her hands now too. 'Yes! So I'm not bleeding from anywhere else? Forgive me while I— Oh, there's nothing. That's brilliant.'

Rudolpho by now had his face in his hands and his back turned towards her. 'I'll tell your brother not to expect you for the rest of the *month*,' he pleaded. 'If you'll just lie back and wait for a *female* attendant to turn up before you go examining any other body parts. I beg you.'

She lay back and swiped at her nose. How had she not felt that? Had she been too mired in righteous indignation to notice a popped blood vessel? 'You said blood. I thought I was miscarrying.'

'If you could wait there in *silence*,' he pleaded even harder.

'What's going on?' said a gruff voice from the doorway, a voice Claudia would know anywhere.

'Oh, hi. You're back.'

'I never left. My departure was delayed by a wounded falcon and I was worried about my wife. I repeat, why is the King's valet in your—*our*—bedroom?'

'Thank God you're back,' muttered Rudolpho. 'She's all yours. She has nosebleed, fever and she's not herself. I've sent for help.'

'I thought I was having a miscarriage, Rudolpho

thinks I've been poisoned by the bath oil, and Cas wants to know when to expect me for lunch.'

'Barking, the lot of you,' Tomas muttered, and turned to the other man. 'Why are you still here?'

'Possessive.' Claudia approved.

Rudolpho strode to the bathroom, reappeared with the Venetian glass bottle of oil in hand. 'I'll be in touch,' he said, and vanished.

'Care to tell me what's been troubling you for *days*?' Tomas asked with an excess of bite. 'Or would you rather I hear it from somebody else?'

Possessive and out of sorts. 'I had a little spotting the other day.' He looked none the wiser. 'Of blood. From down here.' She motioned with her hand and watched all colour drain from his face. 'The doctor said that can be very normal but to take it easy, so I have been. Except now I have a fever and I'm bleeding from my nose and here we are.'

'And where exactly does the poison theory fit into all of this?'

'I cannot be responsible for Rudolpho's wild imaginings. Only mine.'

'You're telling me you thought you were miscarrying and chose not to tell me, and waved me off to work this morning as if this was just another day in the life of the world's most independent woman. Did I not have a right to know?' His voice was getting louder. 'Did you think I wouldn't cope?'

'I didn't know! And I didn't want to worry you in case there was nothing to worry *about*.'

'Because you've got this miscarriage event covered

all by yourself, is that right? Was all your wedding night talk about needing to lean on me sometimes a lie?'

'No!'

'Because I don't see you leaning, Claudia. And I need you to.'

'Not for every little thing! I said that too, on our wedding night.' She swiped at her nose with the side of her hand—it was bleeding again, or maybe it had never stopped. 'Damn.'

'Don't move.' He pointed his finger at her for good measure and went into the bathroom, returning with tissues and a damp facecloth. 'Thinking you might be losing your baby is no small concern. Thinking you might have been poisoned by the bath oil—why haven't you ever raised that as a possibility?'

'Because I doubt it is one.' The wet cloth felt cool against her burning skin as she lay back against the pillow and savoured the temporary relief. 'I'm not that disliked, am I?' Maybe she was. 'I have a nosebleed and a temperature. Or a fever that might have caused the nosebleed. The doctor will shed some light.'

'And the other bleeding?' He turned the rapidly warming cloth on her head over to the cool side. 'What happened there?'

'A little bit of blood on my panties, not much, but I panicked. The doctor wasn't too worried but did say to take it easy for a while. I didn't want to worry you until I had to,' she murmured again. 'I didn't want to lose you.'

'Lose me how?'

She deliberately kept her eyes closed so she wouldn't

have to look at him. 'You only married me because of the baby. I know that. The world knows that.'

'I married you because I'm worthy, and if you think I'd leave you if you lost this baby, you're out of your feverish mind. You *have* to stop working so hard for others! I've asked for this and now I'm begging. Stop! It won't make us love you any less. How can you not know this? Get it through your head!'

Her Tomas was yelling now. It was a sight to behold and somehow it *did* make her feel loved.

She was so screwed up.

'You love me?' she asked quietly. 'Really?'

'*Yes!* Baby or no baby. Whether you love me or not. Regular as sunrise. *Yes!* How can you not *know* this?'

'You never said.'

'I told you on our wedding day. Do you think I'm in the habit of making false vows? Don't answer that. You thought that. And you thought wrong. I've been trying to show you how much I love you ever since. You want to hope you haven't been poisoned,' he added next.

'I *do* hope that,' she told him earnestly.

'Because my vengeance will not be kind,' he added. 'I'm a lovelorn man on the edge.'

Her smile broke through his emotional frenzy, but only because it was blinding. 'I love you, you know that, right? I've only ever wanted to make your life better, never worse. I want…' The temptation to tell him she wanted whatever *he* wanted was *so strong*. She was fighting to stay awake—surely that wasn't normal after a full night's sleep and a morning spent lazing around. 'Tomas?' She reached for his hand and it was warm and big, with pleasing callouses. Not as overheated as she was and surely that couldn't be good for the baby. 'If something really is wrong and you have to choose betw—'

'I choose you,' he interrupted. 'No debate and no apology. I will always choose you. Please don't make me prove it.'

His answer was… 'Acceptable.' Enlightening. 'For now. We may have to have this conversation again once our baby is on the ground and the light of our lives.'

'We are *never* having this conversation again. You're not miscarrying, you've not been poisoned and you're not dying on my watch. Never again, without me going with you. There's nothing else to discuss.'

She sighed and couldn't tell where sorrow ended and delight began. 'I suppose we could consider that settled.' Feverish she might be, but there would be no forgetting that promise. Tomas was perfect in every way and she was a bad wife for not trusting him to be rock-solid there for her, no matter what.

'No more protecting you from pregnancy worries.'

'No more.'

'We can share the panic.'

'We can.'

'I'm really glad you hung around this morning.'

'I'm not a mind-reader. Next time say, *Tomas, would you mind staying with me this morning? I'm not feeling great*. That is all it's ever going to take!'

'Yes, but *not feeling great* is fairly common for me these days. How do I tell the difference between morn-

ing sickness, a bad scallop and a right royal assassina-
tion attempt?'

'I'll ask around. Maybe Ildris will know.'

'You're bonding with Ildris now?'

'No way, nohow and never. But I'm not above in-
stilling overwhelming concern for you in his heart. He
deserves it.'

'I didn't realise I'd married a comic genius masquer-
ading as a madman,' she murmured.

'Didn't you?' he grumbled, right on cue. 'Well, now
you know. Claudia?'

'Mmm?' So weary.

'You can't die again. I won't let you. You're going to
beat this. Whatever it is.'

'I'll do my very best.'

'And I will ever be with you.'

There was no poison in her blood. The bath oil had been
declared safe and Lady Ester had been indignant. The
spotting had stopped but a piece of Claudia's placenta
was flapping. It was all very manageable for a man of
reason capable of exerting great control when needed.

And if that no longer described him in full, Tomas
was altogether on board with fudging it.

He'd called on Casimir and told him to stop using
Claudia as his personal scapegoat.

He'd cornered Ildris and requested, on Claudia's be-
half, more support from the northerners during her complicated pregnancy. Alya lived with them at Aergoveny
now, alongside two other young women from the north,
and three young men from Aergoveny, the younger ones

duly added to the apprenticeship roster, and staying in the west wing of the manor house.

Outreach, Tomas called it. Surrounding Claudia with people who knew and accepted her as her own good self was what Tomas *meant*.

He'd made it happen. Simple.

He'd braced his big body as he'd stood in front of all comers, crossed his arms and reminded every last one of them of all she'd ever done for them and the love she deserved. He'd warned them ever so politely that should they ever feel the urge to use his wife's overarching need to make herself useful for their own benefit they should do so extremely carefully. If anyone broke her, he would break them. No exceptions. He was being very reasonable!

How fortunate everyone agreed.

'I need your help these next few weeks to supervise Alhena,' he said to Claudia one morning as he pulled up a chair to her bedside. There were dozens of chairs in the room and yet not one of them seemed like a useful place to sit. 'She's not immune to one of the male goldens we introduced her to and I want to bring them both in here for you to keep an eye on.'

'You mean in this room?'

'Yes.'

'And you chide me for bringing my work home with me,' she murmured with a roll of her eyes. 'Okay, yes. I'll do it. But only because I like Alhena.'

'Perfect.' He sighed. 'But if she has taken to him, they'll need close observation. That'll take weeks. In here. Under your watchful gaze.'

'Now you're just making stuff up.'

'You noticed. You can always sit and watch the grass grow. I'm trying to be supportive about the fact that you'll be spending these next few months on bedrest until this baby is born. You'll crack unless you have something to do, and I need you whole when the baby comes. You're going to be the most amazing mother, have I mentioned that? Adventurous and unconventional, tender and encouraging. There will be hugs. So many hugs, and falcon jesses. It takes a village to raise a child and I'm all for building one right here around you. We're going to add a table and a couple of comfy chairs by the window, and in the mornings I can push the screens aside and let the mountains in. And we'll put the baby's bed over in the corner, and once she arrives she'll sleep long and well, until we're ready to greet her every morning.'

'Oh, you poor deluded soul, but please continue. Are there tapestries on the walls?'

'Er...yes?'

'Excellent.'

'What else do you want me to set right in our world?' he wanted to know. Big or small, petty, silly or serious— he'd make a deal with the devil if it meant keeping his wife hopeful.

The doctor arrived for her weekly check-up, and asked questions and took Claudia's temperature and blood pressure, then collected a blood sample and a urine sample and finally pulled out her stethoscope and listened to the heartbeat.

Then she sat back on the edge of the bed, arms

crossed, and levelled them both with a no-nonsense gaze. 'Here's the deal. You're too far away from proper medical care here and we need to do some investigating.'

'I can relocate to the palace,' offered Claudia, but the doctor was already shaking her head and Tomas's heart was dropping to his toes.

Just when he'd thought he had everything under control.

But it came with the territory and he was there for it.

'Pack your bags,' the doctor said. 'You're going straight to the hospital.'

From bad to worse and worse again, Tomas paced the hall of the hospital and King Casimir, Ana and Ildris paced with him. He wasn't built for narrow halls and tiny waiting rooms, he wasn't used to this kind of terror. None of them were.

Part of him wished Claudia could see them all falling to pieces at the thought of her absence. She'd know she was loved then, without doubt, rhyme or reason. Her usefulness had nothing to do with it.

He couldn't stop pacing.

He wanted nothing more than to return with her to the mountains.

'You love her,' Ildris murmured. 'I wasn't sure of that.'

'You need to stop talking.'

'Mr Sokolov?' A woman had appeared by way of the door at the end of the corridor.

'Yes.' There was no need for titles here.

'You can see your wife now.'

He looked to Cas. Tomas had no intention of giving up his place for the other man but, y'know… King. 'I'll tell her you're here. I'll tell her you're all here.'

'Go,' said Cas. 'Get in there.'

Everything was so white when it came to hospital rooms and beds. It wasn't soothing, thought Claudia. It wasn't soothing at all, but she was in good hands, the doctor kept telling her. The best hands in the country were here and if she could stay put for even one more week, with her baby in her belly, the baby would benefit. Partial placental abruption was manageable. In her case, continuous external foetal monitoring of the foetal heartbeat was recommended.

No problem.

Whatever she had to do, she'd do it.

The door opened and Tomas stepped in and she willed her heart to stop beating faster at the sight of him. He looked at the machines she was hooked up to, paying particular attention to the heartbeat monitor.

'That's our baby's heartbeat,' she told him. 'She's okay for now.'

'She?'

'Oh. I actually don't know. The technician who did the ultrasound absolutely knows but I didn't ask. She, he, either way, I'll be happy and grateful.'

'I love you,' he said. 'I'll be saying that more often.'

Brilliant.

'I'll be staying here until this baby is born,' she said. 'Doctor's orders.'

Her favourite falconer in the whole wide world digested that news with the shrug of his very capable shoulders. 'Makes two of us. I'll be here when you go to sleep of a night and I'll be here when you wake up each morning. You don't like waking up alone in strange places.'

She looked to the doctor. 'Can that...?'

'Be arranged? Of course. We can move you to a double room with a window view. Of course, there should be no intercourse between now and the birth.' Tomas looked scandalised. The doctor looked apologetic but resolute. 'It is my duty to state that.'

Rock-solid Tomas said, 'Thank you, Doctor,' and looked to Claudia. 'I love you and you need me. Which is the only reason I haven't completely lost my mind yet.'

'I will always need you,' she said.

'Thank you,' he said again. 'That's very useful.'

He was so delicious. 'I'm confident this is going to end well for us.'

'I love you,' he said again. 'It bears repeating. Repetition is very effective in a learning environment.'

'You're the falconer,' she murmured. 'By all means, prime me to fly into your arms. You probably don't even need to use food.'

The doctor snorted and the attendant who'd done the ultrasound covered her smile by way of rubbing her hand across the lower half of her face.

'Moving *on*,' said the doctor. 'I'll go and brief the King and Queen and the northern lord who's out there in the waiting room with them and then see about a room change, and someone will arrive in due course to take down your dietary requirements.'

'No hospital food will be necessary,' said Tomas. 'The palace considers poisoning a high risk. There will be guards. There will be food coming in from outside. You'll meet Rudolpho. He'll organise everything and you will endure.'

'Because they love me to bits.' Saved Tomas having to say it, but he was nodding most seriously.

'Yes. Yes, we do. Isn't it obvious?'

'Very,' said the doctor with a wink in Claudia's direction. 'Claudia, I'll leave it to you to keep your loved ones in check. May I suggest no falcons, no parades, no dinner parties in your room and no press? If you think of anything else I need to ban, let me know.'

'Thank you, Doctor.'

And then it was just her and Tomas, with his mighty heart packed full of love to give. 'You don't really have to stay here with me until I have this baby, you realise. At some point I fully expect you to come to your senses.'

'I don't think so.' Gently implacable was his stance.

'Because you love me?' She could get used to such devotion.

He smiled and it was just for her. 'Now that you mention it, yes.'

EPILOGUE

BABY SOKOLOV MADE her way into the world at thirty-four weeks and six and a half days, by way of Caesarean section. She greeted the world with wide eyes followed by a lusty bellow, and her father was there to hold her and fall in love, and later place her gently to her mother's breast.

It had been a mammoth effort to keep mother and child healthy and thriving these past few weeks, but Tomas had put in more effort for less during his time as a falconer, and every moment had been worth it. There was a potter's wheel in the corner of their hospital room and a view of the city skyline out of the window. They'd made all the plates, bowls and vases they would ever need and every one of them was misshapen.

Their daughter, though, she was perfect, with a shock of silky black hair and eyes just like her mother's. They stared steadily at him as she nuzzled at the breast and finally latched on and wasn't that a sight to fill a heart to overflowing.

'What do we call her?' They'd made a list. They'd made a lot of lists during their time indoors.

'Oreah.'

From the Greek: my mountain home.

'Oreah Alya Ana Sophia Lor—'

'Stop.' They couldn't do that to a child. 'Oreah Alya will do.'

'Oreah Alya Sokolov. She's so beautiful,' Claudia whispered. 'Look at her.'

'I think we should keep her,' he suggested.

'Your father thinks he's such a wit. You'll get used to it. I actually think he'll return to normal once we return him to the mountains.' She leaned closer. 'Too much time in a small room.'

He would show his daughter the mountains soon enough, and the stars in the sky and the falcons. She would meet Silas and Lor, her honorary grandparents. She would be passed around to her aunt and uncle and only years later would she discover that they ruled a small country. She would meet wolfhounds and ponies and sleep in a tent in the far northern mountain passes and think she was on a camping trip. She would groan at his dad jokes and he'd hug her to pieces.

He climbed onto the bed as he'd done so many times these past few weeks, and tucked in behind Claudia so she could lean on him and because loving arms meant safety and safety was important. 'Welcome to our world, little one.' And what a brilliant world it was. 'You're going to love it.'

* * * * *

Were you swept up in the drama of
Stolen Princess's Secret?
Then don't miss these other stories
by Kelly Hunter!

Shock Heir for the Crown Prince
Convenient Bride for the King
Untouched Queen by Royal Command
Pregnant in the King's Palace
Cinderella and the Outback Billionaire

Available now!